Surviving **Job STRESS**

HOW TO OVERCOME WORKDAY PRESSURES

BY

JOHN B. ARDEN, PH.D.

CAREER
PRESS
Franklin Lakes, NJ

Copyright ©2002 by John B. Arden

Surviving Job Stress
EDITED BY DIANNA WALSH
TYPESET BY JOHN J. O'SULLIVAN
Cover design by Lu Rossman/ Digi Dog Design
Printed in the U.S.A. by Book-mart Press

To order this title, please call toll-free 1-800-CAREER-1 (NJ and Canada: 201-848-0310) to order using VISA or MasterCard, or for further information on books from Career Press.

The Career Press, Inc., 3 Tice Road, PO Box 687,
Franklin Lakes, NJ 07417
www.careerpress.com

Library of Congress Cataloging-in-Publication Data

Arden, John B.
    Surviving job stress : how to overcome daily pressures / by John B. Arden.
        p. cm.
    Includes bibliographical references and index.
    ISBN 1-56414-609-X (pbk.)
1. Job stress. I. Title.

HF5548.85 .A73 2002
158.7'2--dc21   2001058286

Acknowledgments

I would like to thank my agent Ed Knappman for finding a good home for this book at Career Press. And to the always pleasant and hardworking people at Career Press including Stacey Farkas, Michael Lewis, Kirsten Beucler, John J. O'Sullivan, and Karen Wolf. Also, to Michael Skolnik for his helpful suggestions on the chapters dealing with anxiety and depression. Finally, last but not least, my wife Vicki for her editorial help, for the drawings used in this book, and patience while I wrote and our two sons Paul and Gabriel.

Contents

Introduction: Stressed at Work? 9

    The Changing Workplace 14

Chapter 1: What Is Stress? 17

    Fight or Flight 17

    Controlled and Uncontrolled Stress 21

Chapter 2: Cold Sweat: Anxiety 27

    Anxiety: What Is It? 27

    The Panic Spiral 29

    Defusing the Anxiety 31

    Medical, Drug, and Non-Stress Causes of Anxiety 34

Chapter 3: Down in the Dumps: Depression 37

    Climbing Out of the Quicksand 38

    Depression and Thinking 40

    Get Active 42

    Medical, Drug, and Non-Stress Causes of Depression 45

Chapter 4: You Are What You Eat 49

    Get Balanced 49

    Getting a Boost or a Crash? 53

    Salt 54

    Nicotine 55

    Caffeine 55

Chapter 5: Taking the Edge Off? 61

    Alcohol 62

    Just a Little Toke? 67

Chapter 6: Harassment 71

    Sexual Harassment 71

    The Tyrant 76

Chapter 7: Human Conflict in the Workplace 79

Those "Other" People 79

Social Shock Absorbers 84

Unraveling "Them" 86

Gossip 89

Chapter 8: Seeing Red 91

Losing Control 92

Neutralizing Anger 93

Road Rage 102

Chapter 9: Job Burnout 105

Chapter 10: Medicines and Herbs 109

Benzodiazepines 109

Antidepressants 110

Herbs 113

Chapter 11: Move and Feel Better 117

Stretching 117

Moving 120

Chapter 12: Surviving Tech Stress 123

Age and Tech Stress 124

Humanizing Tech Work 129

Avoiding Impersonal Communication 131

Surviving High-Tech Surveillance 133

Transcending Tech Fear 134

Telecommuting with Less Stress 136

Juggling the Nanosecond 137

Chapter 13: Super Stress 141

Shock Absorbers 142

The Personality of the Supervisor 143

Balancing the Stress of Supervision 146

Chapter 14: Should You Take Time Off? 149

Avoiding the Black Hole 149

Disability and Workers' Compensation 153

Is It Time to Move On? 158

Chapter 15: Job Fishing 163

    The Big Net 163

    The Interview 165

Chapter 16: Making an Attitude Adjustment 171

    Manage Your Time 171

    Stress Tolerance 172

Chapter 17: Get Some Sleep 177

    Sleep: What It Is and What It Is Not 178

    Insomnia 182

    Factors That Induce Insomnia 184

    Sleep Regimen 186

    Treating Insomnia 189

Chapter 18: Relax 197

    Breathing 198

    Hatha Yoga 199

    The Progressive Relaxation Method 200

    Imagery 200

    Self-Hypnosis 201

    Autogenic Training 202

    Body Scan 203

    The Sigh of Relief 204

    Biofeedback 204

    Meditation and Prayer 207

Appendix: Recommended Readings and Internet Resources 211

Index 215

About the Author 223

INTRODUCTION

Stressed at Work?

JOB STRESS. IF YOU PICKED up this book, you're probably experiencing it. Everyone has in some form at some time. Is it your problem? Is your employer causing it? What can you do about it? This book will help you identify the symptoms of job stress and, more importantly, teach you how to survive it.

For most people, coping with job stress requires making psychological and behavioral changes. Whatever your particular problem with your job, the way you deal with stress will have to change.

So, how do you know if you are one of the millions of people suffering from job stress? You probably know you're stressed, but you may be confused by the symptoms. Or perhaps you don't realize how stressed you really are. Many people respond to stress without understanding how it manifests itself and contributes to a wide spectrum of physical, psychological, and behavioral symptoms. This book focuses upon all three categories. Stress affects your body, your thoughts, your emotions, and the way you interact with people. The table on page 10 lists some of the symptoms usually associated with stress.

If you fail to recognize the symptoms of job stress and take action, your stress is likely to snowball. Consider Sara's case, for example. She was a valued employee. Her department's supervisor relied on her more than he relied on any of her co-workers, especially when there was a deadline. He knew that if he delegated the important work to her co-workers, he risked delays. When Sara was assigned a task, she would complete it well before the deadline.

Physical Symptoms	Psychological Symptoms	Behavioral Symptoms
• Headaches	• Pessimism	• Restlessness
• Back pain	• Forgetfulness	• Irritability
• Loss of appetite	• Boredom	• Bossiness
• Overeating	• Indecision	• Accident prone
• Tense shoulders	• Impatience	• Social isolation
• Diarrhea	• Rigid thinking	• Aggressiveness
• Insomnia	• Depression	• Defensiveness
• Fatigue	• Anxiety	• Suspiciousness
• Frequent colds	• Illogic	• Poor hygiene
• Indigestion	• Apathy	• No sense of humor
• Nervous stomach	• Loneliness	• Easily upset
• Shortness of breath	• Feeling hopeless	• Poor work
	• Wanting to escape	• Absenteeism

Table Intro.1. Symptoms of Job Stress

Recently her supervisor broke his leg while skiing. He called Sara and asked if she could fill in as supervisor until his return the next month. Simultaneously, management announced that all of the department's computers needed to be upgraded and the project would have to be completed within two weeks. Sara knew that not all of her co-workers would make the transition easily. She decided to cancel her family vacation and come in on weekends until the project was completed. The last thing she wanted to do was fail.

She began to lose sleep and caught a bad cold but did not alter her schedule. As she had anticipated, her co-workers did not pick up the slack. Panic that the project would not be completed by the deadline began to well up inside Sara. She started to forget simple computer commands. When the director walked in one day, Sara immediately snapped, "What are you doing here?" He walked out shaking his head. She was so shocked by her behavior that she scheduled a team meeting with her co-workers, but quickly became defensive when one of them asked why they had been called together. She shouted, "I can't do all of this by myself!" Then she found herself saying, "You people want me to fail." They left the meeting looking at one another in disbelief.

Is this the **same** Sara? Where did she go wrong? How could she have steered herself off this collision course? To begin with, she shouldn't have considered it her task alone to complete the project. When the director stopped by, she could have expressed her concerns about the deadline and asked for help. Sara needs to change her tendency to do her co-workers' jobs as well as her own. We'll look closely at these issues in the next several chapters.

Not all job stress comes from within. Many workers experience job stress because of harassment from their supervisors. Consider Michael's case: At the end of his shift one Friday, Michael was called to his foreman's office. After Michael parked his forklift, on the way to the office, his stomach felt upset, so he detoured to the bathroom. As a result he was five minutes late. The foreman began the meeting by saying, "Late again, huh Mike? That seems to be one of your problems."

Michael's heart began to pound and his forehead beaded with perspiration despite the fact that it was 50 degrees in the warehouse.

"Well?" his foreman demanded.

Suddenly Michael began to have difficulty concentrating. All he could think about was how to get out of that office. He managed to respond only by saying, "You wanted to see me."

"Yes, you don't seem to be moving fast enough out there. I told you last week that you need to move faster. But you don't seem to get it. Then you ran a forklift into that crate of cereal. Do you know how much that cost us?"

Michael did not want to sound defensive. He felt he had to be honest. "I was trying to move fast."

"Hey, don't be smart with me! You have a week to get things together."

Michael left the meeting feeling lashed. When he got home he barked at his wife and kids to stay away. But his 5-year-old son ran up to him anyway and tried to show him a drawing he had done.

Michael growled, "Didn't I tell you to stay away!"

His son ran out of the room crying.

What were Michael's options? How could he deal with the mounting job stress and prevent it from affecting his home life? There are several options for a person who is being harassed. Instead of dumping on his wife and kids, he should see his family as a refuge. This is another subject we'll cover in this book.

Job stress can also result from the environment you work in because you waste energy adapting to it. Ask yourself the following questions:

- Is my work environment overly noisy?
- Is it cluttered and/or cramped?
- Is there pollution present in the form of toxic chemicals or trash?
- Is there a lack of ventilation and/or light?

Debra experienced several of these environmental stresses. As she sat down at her desk Monday morning her hands began to shake. There it was again, a pile of auto parts catalogues and a box of half-eaten donuts sitting on what was supposed to be *her* desk. She removed the debris and closed the door in hope of warming up the drafty room. Ever since she had begun working as a bookkeeper for the Fire-O Tire Company, it had been evident to her that no one cared about her comfort. She was perpetually wasting time just trying to locate receipts and purchase orders. Often she had to wear earplugs to cut the noise from the hydraulic wrenches. Lately she had been coming to work late and calling in sick. She decided to tell her manager that she could no longer work under these conditions. To her surprise, the manager was not aware that she was uncomfortable. He made immediate changes by moving her to a different office, away from the noise and with more privacy.

Had Debra not talked to her manager, she probably would have endured more environmentally caused stress. Eventually she might have quit her job thinking that no changes were possible. By speaking up she not only got the support of her manager but also her own office.

Some types of work by their very nature have stress written all over them. There are several occupations that are notorious for contributing to stress-related disorders. These include:

- Air traffic controllers.
- Police officers.
- Emergency room nurses.
- Paramedics.
- Firefighters.

One common factor in these jobs is that workers feel events are often out of their control or beyond their power to change. At any time an event could occur that would require all of their resources to avert a bigger crisis.

Several other structural aspects of work can contribute to job stress. Some may be obvious, while some will surprise you. For example, we all agree that too much work can contribute to stress, but too little work can have the same effect.

The following is a list of work conditions and characteristics that research shows trigger job stress:

- Lack of clear goals, objectives, and responsibilities.
- Lack of support from supervisors or co-workers.
- Much responsibility but little authority.
- Undefined expectations.
- Too many deadlines and time pressures.
- Lack of opportunity to voice complaints.
- Frequent, unnecessary, and unforeseeable obstacles.
- A position in which you have to perform beyond your ability.
- A supervisor who criticizes often and praises rarely.
- Supervisory responsibility.
- Intense and continual pressure.
- Age, sex, or racial discrimination.
- A constant threat of layoff.

Gary experienced many of these problems in his job at the post office. Since his transfer to the back office of the mail room, he found it difficult to determine what his job entailed. Unlike the jobs of mail carriers and sorters, his job was poorly defined. His direct supervisor asked him to count all of the incoming packages with the zip code 94001. At the end of the day, he told Gary that headquarters' staff depended on his figures to calculate funds for the branches. Two weeks later he spent days wandering around the building looking for work. He did not want to complain because he had heard that there would soon be a layoff. Instead, he began to lose sleep, feel drained, and lose enthusiasm for hobbies he once enjoyed. Then he pulled himself together and applied for a transfer in anticipation of the possible layoff. He also asked management if he could be trained to use the new equipment that was being installed in the department. During his off hours, he again began to spend time engaging in his hobbies and seeing friends. His sleep improved and his spirits returned, primarily because he pushed himself to take action.

Had Gary waited for management to provide him with a clear direction he probably would have remained stressed out. But, because he mobilized himself both at work and at home, he left his stress behind.

Being constantly interrupted either by co-workers or by the phone can also wear you down. When you are working on a project and you are interrupted in the middle of a thought, the interruption may trigger a chain reaction of stress symptoms. For example, if you are interrupted for the 10th time while trying to write the same sentence, you may snap a rude comment to the person who last interrupted you and a chain reaction begins. She may say, "Well, excuse me!" and then turn to a co-worker and say, "I don't know what is wrong with him." You will probably feel guilty and embarrassed. This cascade of events only serves to contribute to more stress.

Much of what we experience at work is based on how we interpret things. No two people will interpret the same event in the same way. One person may take the onslaught of new deadlines in stride while you may feel overwhelmed. The chain of events looks something like this:

Events (Deadline for the project has been moved up.)

Beliefs ("This is beyond too soon.")

Emotional Reaction (Surging anxiety)

Human existence is infinitely complex, and because job stress results from complex circumstances we need to look beyond simple explanations and solutions. The physical, psychological, and social aspects of job stress all need to be addressed. In this book, I explore all of the interrelated physical, psychological, and social aspects of job stress in depth.

The Changing Workplace

If you suffer from job stress, you are not alone. Between 1985 and 1990, the proportion of workers identifying themselves as stressed at work doubled. A survey conducted by the National Institute for Occupational Safety and Health (NIOSH) found that 25 percent of people surveyed reported that their job was the single greatest source of stress in their lives. A poll conducted by the International Survey Research Corporation in Chicago in 1998 found that 22 percent of workers report that they worry about losing their jobs.

Do you sometimes feel too stressed to go to work? An estimated 1 million people are absent from work each day because of stress-related problems. More than 250,000 workdays are lost per year because of stress.

Job stress costs American employers between $200 and $300 billion a year. These costs result in diminished productivity, absenteeism, accidents, medical and legal bills, worker compensation claims, and job turnover. The most dramatic costs to employers are represented by industrial accidents; an estimated 60 percent to 80 percent of industrial accidents are stress related.

Job turnover alone can cost companies millions of dollars. Xerox estimates that it costs from $1 to $1.5 million to replace a top executive and approximately $2,000 to $13,000 to replace the average worker.

Companies that have merged with others are more likely to have an increase in disability claims and decreased morale and productivity. The director of NIOSH estimates that all this translates into 1 billion dollars of economic loss per year.

Because of the many corporate mergers, work conditions have deteriorated. Workers are asked to stretch themselves for the new company and to do more with less time and support.

This was precisely the problem faced by Denise. For 10 years she had worked for the Federal Bank. Then it was purchased by the Pacific Bank. Within a week, 100 people were laid off at Federal's 22 branches. Denise found herself with twice the workload and a new supervisor who apparently feared for her own job. Denise began to have panic attacks at work.

Her supervisor ran into her in the bathroom trying to regain composure and asked, "Are you all right?"

Denise responded, "I'm just stressed out."

Instead of providing sympathy and support her supervisor said, "Look, we all are Denise. I just need to know if you are going to be able to cut it around here."

Denise felt foolish for opening up. She expected that her supervisor at least would be sympathetic. Now Denise felt more isolated at work then ever before.

She thought she needed professional help and set up an appointment with a psychologist in her health maintenance organization (HMO). Over the course of the next few weeks, Dr. Workman helped Denise develop an ability to neutralize the panic attacks. Eventually, Denise was able to learn a coping strategy and to find her niche in the new merged company.

What type of job stress do you experience? Have you found that stress is so overwhelming that you have considered quitting or that you have been disciplined for poor performance or insubordinate behavior? Have you just begun to think about how stress influences your life? The first step you will need to take is to recognize the symptoms of job stress, which we'll cover in Chapter 1. With this knowledge, you will be able to identify those symptoms relevant to you and begin to do something to relieve your stress.

CHAPTER 1

What Is Stress?

PEOPLE OFTEN NOT ONLY FEEL overwhelmed by job stress but also bewildered by the wide variety of thoughts, emotions, and physical changes it can produce.

If you do not know how to identify these symptoms, you may overreact in a way that amplifies your stress. To develop coping strategies, you must first understand how stress works on the body and mind.

Fight or Flight

Many years ago Harvard professor Walter Cannon first drew attention to the fight-or-flight response to stress. Our bodies go through a variety of changes when we're subjected to stress. These changes prepare the body to deal with a threat in the same way that our evolutionary ancestors prepared themselves when confronted with a life-threatening situation, such as abruptly facing a wild animal. The body is readied to either defend itself or run away from the threat.

The following list represents the bodily changes that occur when your body pumps adrenaline during a fight-or-flight response:

- Rapid heartbeats get blood flowing to the extremities to ready them for action.
- Rapid and shallow breathing charges up the body and oxygenates the blood.
- Perspiration cools the overheated body.
- Muscles tense to brace themselves for quick movements at any time.
- Attention narrows to focus solely on the danger and prevent distraction.

When you are feeling job stress, this fight-or-flight response often makes it more difficult to cope. Rapid heartbeat, perspiration, and shallow breathing hinder your ability to work. Narrowed attention prevents you from considering all of the options for a complex task.

The fight-or-flight response is an evolutionary artifact that complicates our modern work life. The human nervous system was not designed to be in a fight-or-flight mode for 40 hours a week. If the stress continues, a wide spectrum of symptoms may emerge, including:

- Diarrhea.
- Frequent urination.
- Low self-esteem.
- Difficulty concentrating.
- Hostility and aggression.
- Difficulty making decisions.
- Difficulty coping with distractions.
- Irritability.
- Insomnia.
- Feelings of doom and gloom.
- Skin rashes.
- Changes in the menstrual cycle.
- Low sex drive.
- Mood swings.
- Increased daydreaming.
- Insensitivity to others.

Our nervous system needs a way to turn off the fight-or-flight mode. In fact, our nervous system has two such mechanisms: the voluntary and the involuntary. The latter is "automatic" in that it occurs without conscious control, and it has two branches: the sympathetic nervous system, which regulates arousal, and the parasympathetic nervous system, which controls relaxation.

The arousal branch, or sympathetic nervous system, is responsible for the fight-or-flight response. When charged, it activates the brain chemicals, called neurotransmitters, norepinephrine and epinephrine (adrenaline), making you more alert. A chain of events occurs, including the movement of blood away from your skin, liver, and digestive system toward your heart, muscles, and lungs. It also tells your body to release fats such as cholesterol and triglycerides into the blood stream to promote energy.

Because the liver receives less blood during stress, several problems emerge when the stress is chronic. This is because one of the main functions of the liver is to clear the blood of cholesterol. Chronic stress, therefore, can result in a build up of cholesterol (fatty deposits) in your arteries. Consequently, prolonged stress puts you at greater risk for obstruction in your arteries, which can result in strokes and heart problems.

The relaxation branch, or parasympathetic nervous system, helps you tone down and rest by releasing the brain chemical acetylcholine, which acts to dampen the effects of adrenaline.

The overactivation of the sympathetic nervous system corresponds to the fight-or-flight syndrome, leading to a range of physical problems on the job. These include:

- **Suppression of digestion.** Because a great deal of energy is expended in digestion, stress will suppress digestion to save energy. If stress is chronic, this may cause gastrointestinal problems.
- **Cold sweats.** Your muscles need to cool themselves during the fight-or-flight response. Consequently, if stressed while on the job, you may break out in sweats when it is actually cool in the room, leading others to wonder if you have a fever.
- **Muscle tension.** Any time your body braces for quick movement to either flee or fight, your muscles tighten. As a result, your back, neck, or head may ache.
- **Pupil dilation.** Your pupils dilate to permit broad visual readiness. Consequently, your eyes may have difficulty focusing on details.
- **Shivering and hair-raising.** To maximize blood flow to vital organs, blood is drained away from the skin. Due to the constriction of blood vessels, you may find yourself shivering because without blood flowing to your skin the surface area becomes colder.
- **Rapid heart rate.** To insure that blood is pumped to the extremities, your heart may pump faster. Unfortunately, a rapid heartbeat may spur a panic attack.

The psychological effects of long-term stress can limit your ability to perform well at work. This leads to a self-perpetuating cycle because diminished job performance puts you under more stress. Either you will have more trouble getting the work done or you will be put under greater scrutiny by a supervisor. Then, to compensate, you may hurry up to try to accomplish more. As you hurry, you may make more mistakes, get hurt on the job, or create more work because of inefficiency. You may feel so rushed that you make a clumsy and insensitive comment to a co-worker or supervisor and suffer the consequences for that in addition to what you were already experiencing as job stress. Psychologist Dr. David Lewis, in the *American Psychological Association Monitor* (December 1999), calls this syndrome "hurry sickness."

Many workers experience stress because management insists they compensate for corporate weaknesses by working harder. Employees are asked to work twice as fast, while simultaneously dealing with customer complaints generated by the slipshod products or services that result from trying to do too much, too fast, with inadequate resources.

Anita was one such employee. She had worked as a computer phone support technician for five years. But after the company sold thousands of computers with faulty software the support lines rang off the hook. Customers left on hold for as long as an hour were furious. Instead of adding support staff, the company ordered the technicians to spend less time per call. Anita complied, but began to sweat profusely and shiver at the same time. She thought she was catching a cold but found that her heart was beating faster and her breathing rate was higher. It became harder and harder for her to focus on the computer screen. Her neck tightened and she found that she had to run to the bathroom to relieve herself several times during a shift. She began to make mistakes with customers, and some phoned her boss to complain.

When she was called into her supervisor's office after a shift, she decided to be honest. She declared that she was finding that she just could not work that fast and maintain quality. She knew that her supervisor would be left with the choice of letting her go with no replacement available or agreeing to let her work at a more reasonable pace. She also knew that many of her co-workers were experiencing similar problems.

Because Anita was able to recognize the symptoms and causes of stress, she was able to get her supervisor to confront the root problem, doing herself and the company a favor. Without this knowledge, she might have attributed her mistakes to her own inadequacies instead of to their true cause: unrealistic expectations. By insisting her supervisor face facts, she made it clear that the line workers alone could not resolve the company's fundamental problem.

Controlled and Uncontrolled Stress

In *The Stress of Life*, veteran stress researcher Hans Selye said, "Stress can be avoided only by dying." But, Selye noted, everyone reacts to stress differently. One person may see job stress as a threat to his very existence, while another responds to the same set of circumstances as a challenge. You may be more or less vulnerable to stress than your co-workers.

Selye drew attention to what he called the "general adaptation syndrome" to illustrate how one adapts to stress. He described three stages:

1. Physiological alarm.
2. Adaptation to the stress.
3. Exhaustion.

During the alarm phase, all of your resources are put in hyperalert mode to deal with the impending threat or denial. Many of the fight-or-flight response characteristics come into play during this phase.

In the adaptation phase, you struggle to muster your psychological and physiological resources to come to some resolution to the stress. You may narrow your attention to a particular situation at work that contributes most to job stress.

The exhaustion phase comes when you either complete the task or give up. This is the breakdown phase. After an extended period of time dealing with job stress, you may find yourself no longer able to muster the energy to deal with it. As a result, the immune system also becomes depressed, and you may catch a cold.

There are healthy and unhealthy ways to deal with stress. Ideally, you want your body to adapt to the stress rather than break down because of it. The following table shows opposing lists representing two different ways of dealing with short-term stress, one adaptive, one maladaptive:

Adaptive	Maladaptive
• Mobilization of energy.	• Energy depletion, lethargy.
• Increased cardiovascular tone.	• Hypotension, hypertension.
• Suppression of digestion.	• Ulceration, colitis.
• Suppression of growth.	• Psychogenic dwarfism.
• Suppression of Reproduction.	• Low libido, impotence.
• Suppression of the immune system.	• More colds and flu.
• Sharpened thinking.	• Neuronal death.

Table 1.1. Dealing with Short-Term Stress

Researchers have tried for decades to identify which type of people are most prone to respond badly to stress. Many years ago two cardiologists, Mayer Friedman and Ray Rosenman, coined the term "Type-A." They established a connection between a particular type of behavioral pattern (Type-A) with a higher incidence of heart disease. Type-A people tend to be more aggressive, hostile, and seemingly always in a rush. Research has shown that Type-A behavior contributes to stress-related diseases. The "Type-B" personality is far more adaptive and healthy. Type B people are relaxed and take life in stride. They do not overreact to stress but meet it by trying to approach their goals at a comfortable pace.

Researchers have found that stress can cause the levels of a brain chemical called noradrenalin to rise. Stress also causes chemicals called glucocorticoids, including cortisol, to be sent throughout your body after enduring stress. Cortisol is sometimes referred to as the "stress hormone." It regulates carbohydrate metabolism, blood pressure, and body temperature while suppressing cytokine, a key element of your immune system. That's why it is quite common for people who have experienced a great deal of stress to catch a cold. You can see the stress chain of events on the facing page.

Because many people have trouble recognizing the physical symptoms of stress, they go to their doctors for relief. It has been estimated that 75 to 90 percent of visits to primary care physicians are for stress-related problems.

Below are some of the most common physiological complaints presented at the doctor's office that are stress related:

- Headaches.
- Back pain.

The Stress Chain of Events:

Experienced Stress
(For example, the boss tells you to work harder.)
↓
Sensory recognition of the stress by the higher centers of the brain
↓
Information travels down from the cortex to the limbic system
(the emotional brain)
↓
Hypothalumus—Corticotropic Releasing Hormone (CRH)
↓
Pituitary Gland—Adrenocortocotropic Hormone (ACTH)
↓
Adrenal Glands
↓
Cortisol
↓
Lowered immune system
↓
Catching a Cold

- Sexual disorders.
- Skin problems.
- Asthma.
- Digestive and gastrointestinal disorders.
- Dizziness.
- Ringing in the ears.
- Diarrhea.
- Insomnia.
- Bruxism—grinding of the teeth at night.
- TMJ—temperomandibular joint pain—jaw pain.
- High blood pressure.
- Coronary heart disease.
- Herpes—mouth sores.
- Migraine headaches.
- Peptic ulcer.

Your body may react to stress differently than your colleague's body even though you face exactly the same stresses at work. You may channel your stress to your gastrointestinal track and have diarrhea, stomachaches, or decreased appetite. He may experience more headaches, neck, or shoulder tension. You may experience racing thoughts and free-floating anxiety. He may experience a sense of zoning out and numbness.

Dr. Israel Posner and Dr. Lewis Leitnor, in the *American Psychological Association Monitor* (December 1999), contend there are two critical factors in whether stress is experienced as overwhelming or manageable. If your stress is predictable and controllable, chances are you will adapt favorably to stress. If it's neither you will feel helpless.

Even if your job is inherently stressful it need not be overwhelming. But when a worker loses a sense of control and the conditions become unpredictable, the stress becomes too much to handle. For example, Carl has been working as a paramedic for 10 years. However, during the past year he has been dispatched to a part of the city plagued by street crime. On several occasions while picking up patients lying on the street with bullet wounds, his ambulance has been shot at. Recently, Carl has been having severe tension headaches and pain in his neck and shoulders. He has also begun to have nightmares.

For relief Carl went to see Dr. Ready, a psychologist, who recognized that Carl was suffering from Post-Traumatic Stress Syndrome as a result of the shootings. As part of his treatment, he taught Carl stress-reduction techniques.

Carl knew that he had been able to maintain a sense of control over most of his career as a paramedic. When he returned to work after taking some time off, he worked out an arrangement with management that recognized that he had done his time in the crime-infested area of town and could perform his job as competently as ever in a quieter neighborhood.

By facing the need to take care of himself, Carl was able to persevere in a type of work that most people would find extraordinarily stressful. He was again able to relish the challenge of the job once he had regained a sense of control and predictability. If you cannot predict when the stressing events will occur, you will constantly remain braced for them and on guard until you snap.

Sometimes co-workers are the source of job stress. More often they provide the antidote, providing friendship and help. Consider

Sue's situation: Sue knew that going to work on Monday morning would be difficult. She had a pile of work waiting for her and knew her supervisor would not send anyone to help. With the deadline for a report in just a few days, she was sure she couldn't finish it on time. She knew that if she did not complete the assignment she would not only be criticized but possibly fail her probationary period.

As she dropped her 6-year-old son off at school she regretted that was her last diversion before she returned to work. The drive to work took less time than she hoped.

When Sue arrived, she went straight to her desk. As she sat down her heart began to beat rapidly. Her hand shook as she turned on the computer. She opened the file on the middle of the desk and began shuffling through the pages. Her hands were moist and she found it difficult to separate the pages. She did not know where to start.

Anne, her co-worker, walked into the office and said, "Hi Sue. How was your weekend?" Upon seeing the pile of work on her desk and Sue's pale face, Anne said, "Oh, can you handle all that alone?"

Sue felt immediately ashamed of herself. Should she tell Anne how overwhelmed she felt? No, she thought. She nodded yes, trying not to make eye contact. She forced a smile, saying, "No problem."

Anne looked confused and said, "Great. I just thought, you may need some...well anyway...see you later."

Before Sue could cry out, "Wait!" Anne was down the hall greeting another co-worker.

Then Sue remembered that once before she had been in a similar position in the past. After a few weeks, she had finally developed the courage to ask for help. By just remembering how she resolved that situation Sue began to feel more at ease. Her heart stopped pounding. She found herself better able to focus on the file in front of her. She identified a few tasks that could be delegated and she outlined what needed to be done. Then she walked down the hall to find Anne.

Sue almost let help and a potential friendship slip away. Yet, as a result of swallowing her pride and reaching out for help, she gained both the assistance and friendship Anne offered.

CHAPTER 2

Cold Sweat: Anxiety

ANXIETY IS ONE OF THE most common emotional reactions to job stress. In its mildest form, anxiety is a feeling of uneasiness; in its most extreme it manifests itself in the form of panic attacks. Nearly all of us experience anxiety in some form or another due to stress on the job. Sometimes it's just a nuisance; at other times, it's paralyzing. This chapter looks at the various types of anxiety and what you can do about them.

Anxiety: What Is It?

Your experience of anxiety will differ from your co-worker's experience. While you may feel shaky and faint, he may feel nauseous and unusually self-conscious. A variety of sensations and symptoms are associated with anxiety:

- Feeling faint, dizzy, or light-headed.
- Trembling hands.
- Sweating (not due to heat).
- Shortness of breath.
- Fear of dying for no apparent reason.
- Feeling of impending doom.
- Diarrhea, nausea, or abdominal distress.
- Numbness and tingling in the hands.
- Parasthesias (tingling of the skin).
- Inability to relax.
- Feeling tense or "on edge."

- Feeling like you are choking.
- Heart beating fast.
- Feeling detached from your body.
- Fear of being alone.
- Extreme self-consciousness.
- Impaired attention and concentration.

There are many causes of anxiety. To deal with it, you must first determine whether or not your anxiety symptoms are connected to a specific stressor such as your job.

If your anxiety did not predate your job stress, it's a good bet that your stress is situational, or job-related. If the situation and your resulting anxiety are addressed promptly, it can be mastered before it becomes a pattern.

If your anxiety goes on for more than six months after the situation changes, it has developed into an enduring pattern. Now, the anxiety has become generalized into a bad habit independent of its original cause.

Another type of anxiety that can flow from job stress is referred to as a "phobia." People with phobias suffer anxiety connected to a specific type of stress trigger, such as talking to people. This is called a "social phobia." If you suffer from a social phobia you probably experience anxiety in situations such as meeting new co-workers or delivering a public speech.

The way to overcome a social phobia is to practice exercises that "recondition" you to gradually become more comfortable with social situations. The more that you see yourself function in the social arena, the less likely you will have a phobic reaction.

An anxiety syndrome referred to as Generalized Anxiety Disorder (GAD) is more complex and difficult to resolve. If you have GAD, you probably feel anxious most of the time. You may regard yourself as a chronic worrier. At work you probably have a tendency to overreact to stress and may torture yourself with "what-if" thoughts throughout the day: "What if the office door is closed when I get there?" or, "How will I be able to face my co-workers?" If you have GAD, you may misinterpret your suffering as stemming primarily from job stress.

Generalized Anxiety Disorder differs from panic disorder and phobias in that the anxiety is similar to chronic pain: it may not go away and it is less intense. The symptoms of GAD may intensify from time to time depending on the situation. For example, even though you may have felt anxious throughout the day, when your boss walks into the room your anxiety peaks.

These are some common symptoms of GAD:

- Muscle tension.
- Restlessness; feeling keyed up or on edge.
- Irritability.
- Mind going blank or difficulty concentrating.
- Easily fatigued.
- Sleep disturbance.
- Feeling like there is a lump in your throat.
- Frequent urination.
- Dry mouth.
- Clammy hands.
- Feeling shaky or trembling.

The most dramatic and frightening type of anxiety disorder is called panic disorder. During a panic attack, which can occur at any time, the sufferer feels an overwhelming rush of anxiety. Panic attacks are very similar to the fight-or-flight response. Attacks can occur at work or be triggered by the thought of returning to work, especially if a person has experienced a great deal of stress on the job.

The Panic Spiral

Many people who are afflicted with panic attacks feel that they come out of nowhere. If you have a panic attack on the job, it may have begun with just a little anxiety. It snowballs into a full-blown panic attack when you overreact to the initial symptoms of anxiety. For example, you may feel nauseous, have a bout of diarrhea, or feel your hands tremble as you go to work, then say to yourself, "Isn't it enough that I am experiencing this job stress? Now my body is falling apart!" Next you begin to panic, "Oh, my God. I've got to get out of here before I go crazy." The chain of events looks something like this:

Stressful cue (For example, seeing your boss.)
Body symptoms develop (Rapid heart beat, dry mouth, shaking, etc.)

⬇

Negativistic thoughts ("I can't do this.")

⬇

Catastrophic reaction ("I'm going to have a heart attack.")

⬇

Full-blown panic attack ("I've got to get out of here!")

If you interrupt this chain of events by shifting your attention away from thinking about your bodily symptoms and questioning your competency, a panic attack can be defused before it snowballs. This is exactly what James learned to do.

As head chef for a recently acclaimed restaurant, James finished the prep work late on Friday afternoon in anticipation of a large dinner rush. He felt a sense of pride in himself but also a surge of stress. With an increase in the number of customers, he wondered if he would be able to maintain the high quality of the establishment's meals.

The restaurant filled quickly and by 6 p.m. a line had formed outside. James felt his heart begin to pound, and he started to hyperventilate. His thoughts began to race and he told himself, "I can't do this! My heart is pounding and I'm going to have a heart attack. What if someone sees me?" He paced around the kitchen trying to decide what to do. Then as orders started flooding in he began to sweat profusely. Instead of facing the first batch of orders he thought, "I'm incapable of working. I can't even walk. My legs are buckling." He struggled to get out the back door for air. Once outside he slowed down his breathing and refocused on the task at hand. He thought that if he took a small bunch of orders at a time he would be able to get through the night.

As a result of his self-defeating thoughts about sweating and a rapid heartbeat, James felt more anxiety. Very quickly that anxiety spiraled out of control. He would have been better off if he had simply acknowledged that the symptoms of anxiety would pass and adapted to the new demands by focusing on breathing, then shifting his attention to brief and discrete tasks, one at a time. He also could have repeated reality-based, constructive thoughts such as:

- "I'm not going to have a heart attack."
- "I'll get through this. These feelings will pass."
- "All I need to do is stop and breathe deeply."

Many classes and treatment groups help people overcome panic attacks by teaching them how to "ride out" the panic. This approach is effective because one of the main problems associated with panic attacks is that people become more anxious as they feel the symptoms of anxiety. Essentially, they panic about panic.

Recognize that there really is nothing to panic about and you will ride out the symptoms of panic. Each time you successfully ride through a panic attack the intensity of the next one will be less severe, and eventually your panic attacks will cease.

Defusing the Anxiety

More than a century ago, Russian physiologist Ivan Pavlov demonstrated that he could condition dogs to salivate when they heard a bell. He did this by repeatedly pairing a bell and food. This process of pairing has come to be known as "classical conditioning."

Anxiety is often nothing more than a conditioned response. After the initial pairing of a stressful event and anxiety, a person may experience anxiety with just a reminder of the event. For example, after experiencing job stress due to work overload, you may experience free-floating anxiety just by being at work, even if your workload has subsided. We can say that the anxiety becomes conditioned to work. When you walk into the building, you may feel a surge of anxiety. You must *recondition* yourself so that you do not feel anxiety at work.

One way to do this is to through "cue-controlled" relaxation. You will need to desensitize yourself to the anxiety-provoking aspects of your workplace and re-sensitize yourself to its positive or at least neutral aspects. You will be substituting positive cues that trigger relaxation for the negative cues that trigger anxiety.

If you usually feel anxious when you approach the front door of your work building then you must recondition the front door. You can start with desensitizing how you approach that door. Go back to the door repeatedly while practicing deep breathing and relaxation until the door becomes a neutral stimulus.

After the door has become a neutral stimulus, continue your exercise until the door becomes a cue for relaxation. In this way you have changed a negative cue that had triggered an anxiety attack into a cue that triggers relaxation.

You may choose to provide yourself with a relaxation cue that you can carry with you anywhere. Try using a ring you wear on your right hand. Perhaps you can tap lightly on the ring and practice relaxation. Later, when at work, you can tap on the ring to remind yourself of the feeling of relaxation. The ring, therefore, can serve as a relaxation "anchor" that brings back those feelings.

Do not limit your goals to reducing the symptoms of anxiety. This would be only a bandage. You will need to examine and do away with "bad thinking" habits that perpetuate anxiety.

There are several bad thinking traps that lead to anxiety. They all share a common tendency to "lock in" expectations of how things "ought to be."

- **Perfectionism**: People who regard themselves as "perfectionistic" set themselves up to disparage the quality of their work. Consequently, they drive themselves into anxiety. Allow yourself to be human, imperfect by definition.
- **Rigidity**: Rigid thinkers have trouble thinking beyond black/white, either/or, and right/wrong possibilities. Rigid thinkers fail to see the shades of gray.
- **Control obsession**: People who feel an intense need to maintain a strict sense of control of the events in their lives set themselves up for constant rude awakenings. We are not in total control of all the events in our lives; we never have been, and never will be. You may be experiencing job stress because you are obsessed with maintaining control over the flow of work and how your co-workers do their jobs.

Our "mood state" affects how we interpret the events and the body sensations we experience. We all make statements to ourselves about what we are experiencing at a given moment. When we are experiencing anxiety those statements are filtered by an anxious state of mind and become self-perpetuating. For example, while at work you may say to yourself, "I cannot stand this anymore," or "This is never going to get any better." These statements actually heighten the anxiety.

In order to combat anxiety, you will need to replace those negative self-statements with coping self-statements. These statements should be based on truisms about anxiety and your job. For example:

- No one ever died of anxiety.
- My body is feeling the anxiety I have about my job but it will pass.
- There is nothing wrong with me.
- I can develop better coping techniques.
- I will survive this anxiety just as I have before.
- These feelings are just a cue to practice my coping techniques.

In addition to accepting the symptoms of anxiety to lessen their impact, you need to focus on other aspects of your life. Redirect your attention away from the anxiety-provoking aspects of your job. In other words, "change the subject." Instead of reacting with anxiety to a particular stress factor at work, shift away from it to another part of your job. By redirecting your attention, you will allow yourself the opportunity to experience more than one emotional response to your work situation.

Redirecting your attention may seem to be an impossible task if your work involves rapid-fire demands and you deal with the public. Yet, consider how Lily was able to meet this challenge:

Lilly had worked as a phone operator for 15 years. During the past two years she had become increasingly anxious. The tempo and flow of calls felt like torture, wearing her down. She braced herself for every incoming call and felt a lump in her throat and a surge of anxiety after she said, "Operator."

A co-worker who was experiencing the same thing told her how she had recently dissolved her anxiety. She told Lily to pay close attention to the different types of voices and the tone of how each person asked for assistance. Lily began to follow her advice and decided she too had an opportunity that few people have, to make contact with hundreds of people. She found that if she was friendly, the tone of the other person seemed to change. She began to experiment with different tones of voice herself. As she went through this process, she found that her anxiety had lessened considerably. She found that instead of dreading each call, she looked forward to the opportunity for another "social experiment."

Lily's shift in attention to her "social experiment" did not slow her down or make her any less productive. Rather, because of this shift in attention she flowed through calls, accepting each new one as another adventure.

Another way to intercept the anxiety spiral is to "externalize" your focus of attention. If you are overloaded with anxiety, you probably pay such close attention to all of the sensations of anxiety that you can't focus on what is important. By redirecting your attention to stimuli outside of yourself, you can break the cycle of escalating fear that fuels anxiety.

For example, instead of focusing on your hand trembling as you open the door of the building at work, or your queasy stomach, listen to the click of the door. When you sit down feel the texture of the chair fabric. When you take a sip of water taste the subtle differences between the water at work and the water at home. Carefully observe the colors or the clothes people are wearing.

Brenda managed to develop this skill. Initially, she found her job as a bank teller quite taxing. She felt a peculiar sense of anxiety half-way through her shift. Her hands trembled as she counted out bills. Each new customer felt like a faceless robber harassing her even more than the previous customer.

Then she decided that she was going to focus on each of her customers' faces and find something attractive about every one of them. She noticed how one of them had auburn hair, which accented her eyes. Another had a gray goatee, which made him look distinguished. Each day she tried this technique and each day she felt just a little less anxious. Soon she regarded herself as having a keen ability to read people's lives just by watching them carry themselves. Anxiety became a distant memory, and she now looked forward to each interaction.

By shifting her attention outside of herself and away from the demands of the customers she was able to neutralize her anxiety. She was able to covert what was the source of her stress into a source of enrichment.

The overall guiding principle is to learn a behavior that is incompatible with anxiety.

Medical, Drug, and Non-Stress Causes of Anxiety

Many medical conditions contribute to anxiety-type symptoms. For example, mitral valve prolapse (MVP) occurs in 5 percent to

15 percent of the general population. Approximately, 50 percent of these people experience chest pains, breathlessness, and palpitation. If a person with MVP were to experience these symptoms and not understand their origin, he may overreact to the physiological symptoms and assume that his job is spurring a panic attack. If you have MVP and job stress simultaneously there is an increased susceptibility to anxiety.

If you have a medical condition that is correlated with anxiety symptoms, you should seek treatment for that condition. Following is a list of some of the medical conditions associated with feelings of anxiety:

- Adrenal tumor.
- Cushing's disease.
- Hypoglycemia.
- Hypothyroidism.
- Meniere's disease.
- Parathyroid disease.
- Post-concussion syndrome.

Anxiety symptoms can also be the result of metabolic and toxic effects of either consuming or being exposed to a variety of chemicals or compounds. For example:

- Exposure to environmental toxins such as hydrocarbons, mercury, and carbon dioxide.
- Withdrawal from alcohol, barbiturates, and benzodiazepines.
- Deficiencies in magnesium, vitamin B-12, potassium, and calcium.

Some people may suffer from hypoglycemia and not know that their anxiety symptoms are the result of low blood sugar. If your blood sugar drops below 50 milligrams per milliliter and you suffer from hypoglycemia you may find that you experience:

- Free-floating anxiety.
- Shakiness.
- Light-headedness.
- Irritability.
- Rapid heartbeat.
- Difficulty concentrating.

These symptoms often occur three hours after eating. If you have hypoglycemia and consume a few candy bars or a few soft drinks loaded with sugar three hours after eating a meal, the symptoms of anxiety will intensify.

People receiving treatment for various medical conditions often experience anxiety. Many medications have side effects that cause anxiety symptoms. Unfortunately, your primary care physician may not warn you of these side effects. Also, you may be taking an over-the-counter medication that has anxiety-related side effects. Following are some of the types of medications that have anxiety-related side effects:

- Asthma medications.
- Nasal decongestant spray.
- Many decongestants.
- Steroids.

Try talking to a pharmacist when you pick up your medication. Pharmacists usually know the side effects of various medications. Always read the medication information sheet that comes with the bottle.

Many jobs may involve environmental irritants that make specific medical conditions worse. If you have a medical condition that is exacerbated by aspects of your job, you have a choice to make. You can either quit or reduce those aspects that make your medical condition worse.

Bill chose to stay with his job. For a year he had worked as a toll taker on the Golden Gate Bridge. Recently he found that within an hour of starting his work shift he was out of breath and panting. He thought he might have asthma and started using nasal sprays. This only intensified his symptoms of anxiety. His hand began to shake as he reached out to take the tolls. He thought that the job was too much for him. His self-esteem plummeted. Then he went to a psychologist who told him that the combination of the car fumes and the nasal sprays were creating his symptoms. He stopped using the nasal sprays immediately and ventilated his tollbooth. Then despite the joking of some of his peers he began to wear a mask. Soon Bill began to feel like his old self.

Because Bill took concrete and practical steps to shield himself from the harmful aspects of his job he was able to keep his position. Perhaps that option is not available to you. If not, consider your health far more important than your job. Being mindful of your health and making appropriate changes will insure that you do not experience needless anxiety, making your job stress worse.

CHAPTER 3

Down in the Dumps: Depression

DEPRESSION IS VERY COMMON AMONG people suffering from job stress. Depression can result in a far more debilitating experience than anxiety. Many people who suffer from depression are unaware of how deeply depressed they have become until they are functionally impaired by it. They can't seem to find the motivation it takes to begin climbing out of the depression. Therefore, it is important to be able to identify the symptoms of depression:

- Fatigue.
- Low sex drive.
- Tearfulness.
- Negativistic thinking.
- Early morning awakening.
- Insomnia or hypersomnia.
- Feeling hopeless or worthless.
- Irritability.
- Rapid weight loss.
- Low appetite.
- Feeling like "going away".
- Social isolation.
- Depressed mood.
- Difficulty making decisions.
- Feeling as if everyone is against you.
- Bleak attitude about the future.
- Bored with everything.

- Former hobbies bring no pleasure.
- Suicidal thoughts.

If several of these symptoms are plaguing you, professional help may be necessary. If you have been thinking of suicide, please call your local mental health center for help immediately. But if you are among the vast majority of people who are depressed, you can do many things to help yourself climb out of the quicksand.

Climbing Out of the Quicksand

Ironically, if you are depressed, you may want to behave in a manner that sinks you deeper into depression. You may want to isolate yourself from people, postpone exercise, and not eat. You may say to yourself, "I am just too tired to exercise," or "I just don't have the energy to be with people now," or "I don't have the taste for food," or "The thought of food nauseates me." If you isolate yourself socially, refrain from exercise, and do not eat, you will become more depressed.

So what should you do? If you want to become less depressed, you are going to have to do things you do not feel like doing. You are going to have to jumpstart yourself by forcing yourself to eat, be with people, and get some exercise. Making an effort to walk or go to the gym may not be easy initially, but the dividends will come shortly after you begin. Forcing yourself to eat is critical. Food is medicine for the brain.

People often say that they have kept the drapes drawn in their house because they "do not want to let the outside world in." Apparently they do not know that low levels of light have been associated with depression. This is not based simply on the idea that having the drapes open means you are open to the outside world. It is a biochemical fact.

Your brain picks up signals from your retina regarding whether it is dark or light outside. If it is dark, your pineal gland will secrete a hormone called melatonin to sedate you and allow you to go to sleep. This is nature's sedative. However, melatonin is a hormone that is very similar in chemical structure to serotonin. When there is an overabundance of melatonin, it competes with serotonin and the levels of serotonin go down. Low serotonin is correlated with depression.

This mechanism is at work in the case of people who are suffering from Seasonal Affective Disorder (SAD). People with SAD often find themselves becoming more depressed during the seasons when there are fewer hours of daylight. A disproportionate number of people in the northwestern United States or northern Europe suffer from SAD because of the overcast skies and shorter days in the winter. I am amazed by the number of times a person vulnerable to depression has told me that they only realized how depressed they had been after they gained more daily exposure to sunlight.

During a period of job stress, you should make every effort to avoid experiencing depression. Keep your drapes open and spend as much time as possible outside. Maximize your exposure to natural sunlight.

People also become depressed because they feel incapable of conquering job stress. Whatever they have attempted to do to remediate their stress at work has not been successful. Professor Martin Seligman of the University of Pennsylvania coined the term "learned helplessness" to describe one very common route to depression. Learned helplessness occurs when a person makes repeated attempts to change a terrible situation and nothing seems to work it. Under these conditions, she will probably become depressed. A classic example is a woman whose husband abuses her. She may attempt a variety of ways to change the situation and "try to make him see the light," but will always fail. Depression is almost always the result.

If your situation at work does not seem to improve despite your efforts to change it, you will probably grow to feel hopeless and depressed. Just as that abused woman finds that she cannot change the marriage and the only way to feel better is to get out, you too may need to make the same decision about your job. Fortunately, you are not married to your job.

To overcome depression:

- Work on problem solving. For example, set short-term goals.
- Increase activities that are productive and give you pleasure. Seek entertainment by going to a movie, a concert, or exploring outside activities.
- Learn how to be assertive. Take a class in assertiveness training.
- Debate irrational ideas.

Depression and Thinking

How you think has a dramatic effect on how you feel emotionally. Depression is fueled by "thinking errors." During the past 30 years, several common thinking errors have been identified:

- **Polarized Thinking**: Black and white, all or nothing, good or bad, wonderful or rotten. This is how a polarized thinker characterizes any given situation. Because of your recent job stress, you may now feel that your job is the most stressful imaginable. Therefore, you find your job depressing.

- **Overgeneralization**: If you take one unfortunate incident that occurred at work and jump to conclusions about the entire job, you will be overgeneralizing. For example, your co-worker may say something rude to you one day, though he has never been rude before. You now think he is a completely rude person and you find him depressing to be around.

- **Personalization**: You may interpret every glance or comment made by co-workers as a negative reflection on you. If your boss, lost in thought, walks past you and does not bother to say hello, you take it as a personal affront. Your job stress is intensified because you feel worthless in the eyes of others.

- **Mind Reading**: You may assume that you know what your co-workers are thinking. During a staff meeting your supervisor comments that everyone must work harder. You assume that all of your co-workers are thinking that you have not been carrying your load.

- **Should and Should Nots**: You may make rigid and inflexible rules (shoulds and shouldn'ts) for yourself that provide you with little flexibility to adapt to today's complex work environment.

- **Catastrophizing**: You may perceive any event as a major catastrophe or a sign of one on the way.

- **Emotional Reasoning**: You may base your opinions on how you feel. If you feel depressed, most of your thoughts about work will be negative.

All of these thinking errors set you up for seeing only the negative aspects of your job. By adopting any of these thinking errors as your own you will limit your options. You will perpetually view your life at work as doomed to failure.

If your job has changed recently you must avoid negativistic thoughts. Negativistic thinking will depress you and limit your ability to adapt to the changes within your job. Bernard fell into this trap. During the past few months, Bernard has been watching his sales plummet. Though his co-workers were experiencing the same decline in sales he felt that his decline was a drain on the store. He began to think his peers were complaining about him behind his back. Wondering if he should resign for the sake of the store, he became sullen, irritable, and lethargic. Bernard talked to his wife about his predicament, and she suggested that he meet with his co-workers. At first he reacted by saying, "I can't talk to them. I will look stupid!" In thinking about it he realized he had nothing to lose. To his surprise, when he talked to them he found that they too had been feeling badly about their lowered sales. Bernard felt a strong sense of relief. He then proposed that they work together to develop a plan to market the store.

Had Bernard kept to himself and not challenged his negativistic thoughts his depression and job stress would have worsened. But because he did challenge those beliefs by talking to his peers, an entire new set of options opened up for him.

Realistic thoughts can crowd out negative thoughts. These realistic thoughts address the job stress. For example:

- I can cope with the job.
- I will take one day at a time.
- I am doing the best I can and that is all I can do.
- I can accept myself for who I am.

If you cannot acknowledge or praise yourself for your accomplishments at work, do not complain that others can't either. This is not to say that you should exude arrogance or boastfulness about your accomplishments. The point is that by acknowledging your accomplishments internally you will not feel the need to constantly look for it in the eyes of others.

Get Active

The best prescription for depression is action. Inaction leads to more depression. You should increase your social contacts and engage in pleasant, productive activities. People who are depressed often say, "I don't feel like being with other people, or doing anything." They may complain, "If I do the things you ask, I will just be going through the motions."

But people who are stressed and depressed complain that they do not "feel like" making any contact with people. It is common to hear people say, "I don't want to put on a happy face and pretend to be someone I'm not."

If you feel guilty because you do not want to "dump" your problems on your friends or relatives, think again. You do not have to tell them how depressed you are about your job. Just being with them will be enough.

The 12-step programs have a nice little jingle: "Fake it until you make it." In other words, engaging in these activities will prime the pump, or get you jumpstarted. Even if you derive just five minutes of pleasure by spending three hours with your friends, you will have gained more than the zero hours that you would have gained by hiding out at home and wallowing in depression.

Social contact is important because we are social beings. If you withdraw from others when depressed because you do not feel like being with people, you will create a vacuum, a void that you will fill with self-loathing and more depression.

Rather than cut yourself off from people you need to take advantage of what social contacts you do have, even though you may not feel like it. Consider this interaction with others to be "social medicine." Although you may not feel like calling a friend, take the plunge! In the long run you will feel much better after spending time with others.

It has long been shown that people who have a broad-based social support system live longer, recover from illnesses more quickly, and get sick less than people with few social contacts. The same goes for recovering from job stress. Our social interactions help us feel wanted, appreciated, and accepted.

In study after study it has been shown that people who are lonely and isolated suffer from more mental illness, particularly depression.

By simply increasing your contact with people, you decrease the chances of being susceptible to mental illnesses.

The bottom line is that staying at home and remaining isolated socially will perpetuate your feelings of depression. Loneliness is associated with higher levels of depression, a depleted immune system, and suicide. In contrast, increasing your social contacts will help you build the emotional support to bridge the depression.

The threat of layoff from your job can trigger feelings of depression and social isolation. This is what happened to Carol. She had enjoyed a variety of friendships until she was threatened with a layoff. She fell into a depression and withdrew from all of her friends. Despite the fact that several people asked her to dinner parties and out to lunch she declined, saying to herself, "I don't want to burden anyone with my troubles." Carol became more depressed sitting in her living room with her drapes drawn. She watched television hour after hour and found herself crying during any scene remotely reflecting sadness. Finally, becoming frustrated with her decline, she began to take walks and call friends. As she allowed herself to spend more time with friends, she gradually became less depressed. At last, she was able to make a decision about where to look for work in anticipation of the potential layoff.

Had Carol continued to isolate herself socially, her depression would have deepened. Instead, she jarred herself out of depression by spending time with friends. These social contacts helped to spring her back into action.

If you engage in the pleasurable activities you once enjoyed in the past, you will remind those parts of yourself that there is life outside of job stress. By forcing yourself to enjoy your old hobby even for a few minutes, you will reawaken part of yourself. These enjoyable feelings, however small, should be cultivated like a garden gone fallow.

Don't trick yourself by saying: "I'll start doing pleasurable things when I feel better." Use your old hobbies as a way to jumpstart yourself. That is exactly what Fred did. After being laid off from his pipefitting job, Fred sank into depression.

He told his wife and friends that he would prefer to be alone. He used to enjoy going fishing with his friend Mitch. When Mitch called to arrange a time for the next outing, Fred declined. Fred stayed home and became more depressed. Finally, his wife talked him into calling

Mitch back. Once he started fishing again, the clean air and the camaraderie began to rekindle a sense of optimism. Within a week he began to look for work.

If Fred had waited for the depression to clear before he went fishing again with Mitch, his depression would have lingered. Going fishing provided Fred with a way to pull himself out of the rut of depression.

If you engage in a productive activity you will begin to feel worthy and useful. So often, people who are depressed due to job stress feel worthless. Engaging in an activity that helps others or working toward your goals will instill self-confidence and a feeling of independence.

Some jobs can deplete your sense of feeling worthwhile. This is especially the case if you work for a supervisor who is short on praise and generous with criticism. Betty found herself in this predicament.

Betty worked as an administrative assistant for the past year for a man who showed little appreciation for her work. She found herself feeling worthless and her self-esteem began to sink. She became tearful and despondent.

For years a friend tried to talk her into volunteering to serve food at the local homeless shelter. Betty felt that she was too tired for such an undertaking. But the next time her friend asked her to go with her, Betty agreed because she was convinced that she needed to pull herself out of the downward spiral. She said to herself, "I'm just going to see what it is like." To her surprise she felt energized by the experience. She began to feel worthwhile and a strong sense of compassion began stirring in her. Her experience at work became a secondary experience and soon she decided to apply for a transfer.

By helping others Betty helped herself. She rekindled the dormant parts of herself and took back what she allowed her supervisor to take away. As a result her depression lifted and she was able to move on with her life.

It has long been shown that support groups also provide a healthy effect. People who feel supported by others who have also been treated for cancer, heart disease, or alcoholism have been shown to have a far better recovery rate than those who remain isolated. If positive benefits can occur with these diseases, imagine what support can do for job stress.

Support groups are extremely helpful to people who are experiencing job stress. Because many people who experience job stress feel lonely and isolated, support groups provide an opportunity to resolve the social deprivation.

It is not uncommon for someone to say, "Why me? Nobody can understand what I'm going through." Support groups give their participants reassurance that they are not alone. Other people have gone through some of the same experiences. Support groups also give their participants the feeling that "people understand."

For the past several years I have heard people in my job stress group spontaneously say, "I felt so alone, like no one understood me. It's so good to see that there are other people who know how it feels to go through this job stress. I don't feel alone anymore."

In Chapters 4 through 7, we will explore how nutrition, substance abuse, medication, herbs, and human conflict affect depression. While addressing those issues, also keep in mind the following activities and guidelines when combating depression derived from job stress. Try to do all of the following:

- Exercise daily.
- Eat a balanced diet and avoid sugar.
- Avoid alcohol.
- Broaden your social support system.
- Rekindle or explore new hobbies.
- Remind yourself of your accomplishments at work.
- Use and tap into whatever spiritual beliefs you have.
- If you are going to watch television or movies, watch comedies or uplifting programs.
- Set small goals for yourself and reward yourself after each accomplishment.

Medical, Drug, and Non-Stress Causes of Depression

There are many causes of depression. Though you may be feeling that your job stress is contributing to depression, it is always prudent to rule out other causes. In fact, many physical illnesses have been associated with causing depression (see Table 3.1).

- Anemia.
- Cushing's Disease.
- Diabetes.
- Infectious Hepatitis.
- Congestive Heart Failure.
- Tuberculosis.
- Asthma.
- Mononucleosis.
- AIDS.
- Addison's disease.
- Multiple Sclerosis.
- Hypothyroidism.
- Premenstrual Syndrome.
- Rheumatoid Arthritis.
- Syphilis.
- Lupus.
- Uremia.
- Ulcerative Colitis.
- Malnutrition.
- Influenza.

Table 3.1. Illnesses that cause depression

If you are receiving treatment for another medical problem, the treatment itself may have side effects that include depression. Medications are not magic bullets. That is, they do not act solely upon the specific area targeted. For example, if you have high blood pressure, your primary care physician may prescribe a medication such as Inderal. Though Inderal lowers blood pressure, it is also correlated with inducing depression. I have often seen patients who are prescribed Inderal or some medication similar to it who were never told that the medication could possibly have a range of side effects including depression. Table 3.2 lists some medications commonly associated with causing depression.

Anti-anxiety drugs	Diazepam	Valium
	Chlordiazepoxide	Librium
	Lorazepam	Ativan
Anti-parkinson drugs	Levodopa	Dopar
Antihypertensives	Propranolol	Inderal
(for high blood pressure)	Methyldopa	Aldomet
	Reserpine	Serpasil, Sandril
Birth Control Pills	Clonidine	Catapres
Corticosteriods	Progestesterone Estrogen	Numerous brands
and other hormones	Cortisone acetate	
	Estrogen	Cortone
		Evex, Menrium, Femest
	Progesterone	Lipo-Lutin,
		Progestasert,
		Proluton

Table 3.2 Depression-Inducing Drugs

Whether or not your feelings of depression have been exacerbated by a medical condition or medications, you need to minimize the problem by working with your doctor, so that you can get out of the dumps. Even though you may feel too depressed to get mobilized, you have to anyway. You don't have a choice, unless you want to continue feeling rotten. You still need to take action and do those things that will eventually pull you out of depression.

CHAPTER 4

You Are What You Eat

JOB STRESS CAN DISTURB YOUR appetite. Through the years I have seen people who have experienced job stress also have a marked decrease in appetite. Food can be one of the furthest things from your mind if you are tormented by a boss who is harassing you or overwhelmed by a demanding workload. You may think food is a luxury for better times, and may say to yourself, "I know it's not good for me to not eat, but I just don't have the taste for it," or "Maybe it would be good to lose weight anyway; I'll just get to it when I feel better." However, worse times are yet to come if you do not maintain an adequate diet. Maintaining a balanced diet will improve your ability to deal with job stress.

If you are experiencing job stress, it is critical that you maintain a balanced diet. It may be hard to believe, but a poor diet can result in a worsening of job stress. If you want to maintain balanced moods and clear thoughts, you will need to eat three balanced meals a day. The last thing you want to do is to misperceive what is going on to you at work and overreact because of imbalances in moods and unclear thoughts.

Get Balanced

You are a biological being and what you eat has a major effect on your biochemistry and how your brain functions. Because your brain is the highest energy consumer of any organ in your body, any change in your food intake will have a major impact on its ability to function.

The food that you eat is fuel for your brain. If you deprive your brain of fuel, it won't be able to produce balanced thoughts and

49

emotions. Your job stress will intensify because your thoughts and feelings become distorted, exaggerated, and unstable.

It's not enough to eat. *What* you eat has a big effect on the biochemistry of your brain. The amino acids that are found in most foods are crucial building blocks for the brain chemicals we refer to as neurotransmitters. Without an adequate supply of neurotransmitters your brain will not be able to function in a balanced manner and produce balanced emotions and thoughts. These neurotransmitters play a major role in the operation of your brain. We know that there are at least 40 different types of neurotransmitters in the brain, but they are not made through Immaculate Conception.

Neurotransmitters are formed by synthesizing specific amino acids that you take into your system when you eat. For example, L-Glutamine is an amino acid found in foods such as almonds and peaches, and when digested your body uses it to synthesize into the neurotransmitter called GABA. Each neurotransmitter has specific function; GABA is very involved in your ability to stay calm. Consider Table 4.1:

Amino Acid	Neurotransmitter	Effects
L-Trytophan	Serotonin	Improves sleep and calmness and mood
L-Glutamine	GABA	Decreases tension and irritability
L-Phenylalanine	Dopamine	Reduces anger and increases feelings of pleasure
L-Phenylalanine	Norepinephrine	Increases energy, feelings of pleasure, and memory

Table 4.1. Functions of Neurotransmitters.

Amino acids are the building blocks of proteins, and there are a variety of foods containing them. Table 4.2 lists foods that are the richest sources of three of the amino acids.

L-Trytophan	L-Phenylalanine	L-Glutamine
• Turkey	• Peanuts	• Eggs
• Milk	• Lima Beans	• Peaches
• Shredded Wheat	• Sesame Seeds	• Grape Juice
• Pumpkin Seeds	• Chicken	• Avocado
• Cottage Cheese	• Yogurt	• Sunflowers
• Almonds	• Milk	• Granola
• Soybeans	• Soybeans	• Peas

Table 4.2. Foods Rich in Amino Acids.

It has been noted that stress depletes the supply of B and C vitamins, as well as potassium. Therefore, it is a good policy to eat foods rich in these elements and perhaps even use vitamin supplements.

Vitamins are not only important as building blocks for the body, but when you are deprived of them, you can experience specific deficits in your ability to think clearly. In Table 4.3 you will find some of the major consequences of deficiencies of B vitamins.

Low B-1	Low B-2	Low B-6	Low B-12	Low Folic Acid
• Decreased alertness • Fatigue • Emotional instability • Decreased reaction time	• Trembling • Sluggishness • Tension • Depression • Eye problems • Stress	• Nervousness • Irritability • Depression • Muscle weakness • Headaches • Muscle tingling	• Mental slowness • Confusion • Psychosis • Stammering • Limb weakness	• Memory problems • Irritability • Mental sluggishness

Table 4.3. Vitamin B Deficiencies.

Vitamins have a direct effect on brain chemistry. The B vitamins, for example, influence the manufacture of specific neurotransmitters:

• B-6 is needed for the manufacture of dopamine through the amino acids of phenylalanine and tyrosine.

• Thiamin (B-1) is needed for GABA synthesis.

There are several natural sources of vitamins. Table 4.4 lists foods that you can find as natural sources of B Vitamins.

B-1	B-2	B-6	B-12	Folic Acid
• Oatmeal • Peanuts • Bran • Wheat • Vegetables • Brewers yeast	• Liver • Cheese • Fish • Milk • Eggs • Brewers yeast	• Wheat germ • Cantaloupe • Cabbage • Beef • Liver • Whole grains	• Eggs • Liver • Milk • Beef • Cheese • Kidneys	• Carrots • Dark leafy vegetables • Cantaloupe • Whole wheat

Table 4.4. Sources of B Vitamins.

A poor diet has long been associated with contributing to health problems. If you suffer from health problems while you are experiencing job stress, those health problems will add to your job stress.

The combination of poor diet and health problems will further deplete your ability to absorb important vitamins and minerals that can help you deal with job stress.

Stress has been shown to affect the level of cholesterol in your body. Because high cholesterol is associated with increased risk for cardiovascular problems, you should watch your cholesterol intake. There are two types of cholesterol: high density (HDL) and low-density (LDL) cholesterol. While HDL cholesterol clears excess cholesterol from artery walls, LDL cholesterol builds up on artery walls. Though you cannot eat "good" HDL cholesterol because it is formed only in your body, you can watch your fat intake, which affects cholesterol. It has been found that saturated fats increase LDL and polyunsaturated fats increase HDL. Therefore, you will want to avoid foods with LDL in favor of foods with HDL:

Foods High in Saturated Fats	Foods High in Polyunsaturated Fats
Butter	Safflower oil
Meats	Sesame oil
Egg yokes	Soybean oil
Coconut oil	Fish
Palm oil	
Whole milk	

During periods of job stress, you may not want to eat. That's what happened to Sandy.

After being laid off from her job at the Great Basin Power Company Sandy had difficulty finding stable work. She managed to earn some money by working for a temporary secretarial service, moving from site to site, but she was constantly concerned about being called back the next day. As a single mother, she worried that she would not have enough money to get through the month. She began to lose her appetite, then decided not to push food on herself to save money. Her concentration level dropped and her sleep became troubled. On a few occasions she made clerical errors and was harshly criticized by the manager of the site. Finally she was sent somewhere else but told by her placement officers to "watch what you do."

Sandy felt humiliated and even more concerned that there would be no work for her in the coming weeks. She became convinced that her options were few and the future bleak. Then her best friend took her out to lunch on Saturday and convinced her to see a vocational counselor at the local community college. In addition to charting a new plan to find a full-time permanent position, the counselor convinced her to eat three meals a day and exercise regularly. Slowly, Sandy was able to regain a sense of hope. After one month she was able to find a permanent position.

Had Sandy not straightened out her diet she probably would have had difficulty dealing with the stress of the job search. So what is a balanced diet? Nutritionists, medical professionals, and the Senate Select Committee on Nutrition and Human Needs recommend the following guidelines:

- Eat more fruit and vegetables.
- Replace foods with processed white flour with complex flour, such as whole wheat.
- Eat less red meat.
- Minimize your consumption of eggs, butter, and margarine.
- Minimize foods with salt.
- Use low fat milk and cheeses instead of whole milk and cheeses.

Getting a Boost or a Crash?

Consuming foods with processed sugars may make you feel better for a few minutes, but there is a high price to pay for that momentary boost. Basically, what goes up must come down. Here is how it works: Your body's pancreas releases insulin to counterbalance the high sugar level. Therefore, after the momentary sugar high you will experience an energy dip, or crash. In other words, instead of going back to the level of energy you felt prior to the sugar high, you fall lower than baseline. To make matters worse, the crash is agitated by the feelings of nervousness. Thus, the end result is nervous depression.

Sugar is a pure carbohydrate that has no minerals, vitamins, or enzymes to aid in its digestion. Thus, when sugar is consumed, it takes nutrient supplies such as B vitamins from parts of the body. As noted earlier, deficiencies in B vitamins cause a variety of problems including anxiety, depression, and difficulty concentrating.

It is not uncommon that people who have consumed too much sugar also overreact to stress. In addition to feeling on edge, people who are crashing off of sugar find themselves irritable and have difficulty concentrating.

I have seen numerous patients who have binged on foods with sugar, such as cookies or candy bars. Not surprisingly, many complain that they have had a difficult time sleeping and are plagued by anxiety and depression. When I tell them about the ill effects of sugar they quit and feel immediate relief.

You may be one of those people who think you need a "boost" of energy to deal with the demands of job stress. You may feel worn down and need something to give you enough energy to get through the day. Candy, cookies, or soda gives you a momentary boost. But you pay a price that outweighs the benefit.

Fran fell into this trap. During her effort to look for a new job she found herself relying on a sugar boost. It got so that she carried candy bars with her throughout the day for a little perk of energy. However, she found herself actually becoming fatigued, anxious, and depressed. Then she developed panic attacks. After I told her to quit the sugar she found her energy level bouncing back and her mood clearing. Her panic attacks subsided entirely.

Had Fran continued to rely on candy for a boost of energy, she probably would have become so depressed that she no longer could endure the stress of looking for work. Her job search would have been put off because of her anxious depression.

Salt

Excessive salt can also be detrimental to coping with stress. If you consume excessive amounts of salt, your body will deplete itself of potassium. Low potassium has been correlated with an increase in anxiety.

People who are under considerable stress or those who drive themselves too hard may develop hypertension. Salt can exacerbate hypertension; it raises blood pressure because it causes fluid retention, which adds stress on the heart and circulatory system. High blood pressure is associated with feelings of "being on edge."

If you are treated for high blood pressure, you may be given a medication such as Propranolol that in addition to lowering blood pressure also makes you depressed. But what if high blood pressure is an avoidable medical problem that can greatly complicate your ability to deal with job stress? If you have high blood pressure that can be managed by lifestyle changes such as lowering your salt intake, you can avoid the depressing effects of hypertensive medication.

Nicotine

Some people begin to smoke or relapse while experiencing job stress. The irony is that nicotine actually increases stress. Though you may initially feel calmer, the effect of nicotine is activation, not relaxation, because the highly addictive receptor sites in the brain receive a "fix." Nicotine actually increases breathing rates, heart rate, brain waves, and stress hormones.

Smoking also increases LDL cholesterol. As noted earlier, high LDL cholesterol increases the risk of cardiovascular problems such as high blood pressure, which can contribute to low stress tolerance.

Caffeine

Caffeine depletes B vitamins (especially thiamin) and raises stress hormones. Large amounts of caffeine put your body into a prolonged state of stress and hyperalertness. Thus, drinking a significant amount of caffeinated drinks is analogous to drinking liquid anxiety. In fact, there is now a diagnostic category called caffeinism. If a person consumes in excess of 250 milligrams of caffeine (2-3 cups of brewed coffee—see Table 4.5 on page 56), he may experience a range of problems, including:

- Nervousness.
- Restlessness.
- Excitement.
- Flushed face.
- Diuresis—feeling that you have to urinate all of the time.
- Gastrointestinal disturbance.
- Muscle twitching.
- Rambling flow of speech and thought.
- Cardiac arrythmia or tachycardia.
- Periods of inexhaustibility.
- Insomnia.

Caffeine Content in Various Sources

Sources	Amounts in Milligrams
Coffees (8 ounces)	
Drip	88-280 (Depending on to what degree it is roasted.)
Percolated	27-64
Decaffeinated	1.6-13
Tea	
Black	45-78
Green	24-56
Delong	20-64
Darjeeling	45-56
Instant	40-58
Soft Drinks (12 oz.)	
Jolt	70
Mountain Dew	55
Coca Cola	30-45
Dr. Pepper	30-45
Cocoa and Chocolate	
Baking Chocolate	18-118
Sweet Chocolate	5-35
Milk Chocolate	1-15
Chocolate Bar	4
Cocoa (8 oz.)	16-56
Medications	
Appendrine	100
Anacin	32
Aspirin	3
Aqua-Ban	100
Aqua-Ban Max.	200
Bromo-Seltzer	32
Cafergot Cope	100
Coryban-D	30
Darvon	32.4
Dexatrim	200
Dietac	200
Dristan Decongestant	16.2
Duradyne-Forte	30
Excedrin	65
Empirin	32
Fiorinal	40
Migral	50
Midol	32
Nodoz	32
Soma Compound	32
Vanquish	32
Vavarin	200

Table 4.5. Caffeine Content in Common Sources

If you have five or more of these problems, you should cut your caffeine intake. If you have these symptoms and also consume high amounts of caffeine, your problems may be more the result of caffeinism than it is job stress. Caffeine can compromise your ability to deal with job stress because of the needless anxiety produced by it.

Caffeine intoxication can cause restlessness, panic attacks, diarrhea, stomach pain, rapid heartbeat, ringing in the ears, and trembling. After the caffeine wears off there is a crash, which can result in headaches, fatigue, and difficulty concentrating.

Caffeine raises the levels of the activating neurotransmitters dopamine and norepinephrine. Norepinephrine is closely related to adrenaline. Thus, when you consume a great deal of caffeine, you may feel like you are adrenaline charged.

It has been shown that caffeine dampens the level of adenosine, a neurotransmitter that helps you calm down and become sedated. Caffeine is chemically shaped like adenosine and sits on its receptor site in the brain, thus blocking its absorption. Therefore, high levels of caffeine, especially if consumed in the afternoon or evening can promote insomnia and a poor quality of sleep. Caffeine has been found to suppress the deepest sleep (Stage 4 sleep), which is the most restful stage of sleep. Stage 4 sleep recharges your immune system, and people who don't get enough stage 4 sleep get more colds and wake up feeling less rested.

Caffeine also suppresses Rapid Eye Movement (REM), or "dreaming" sleep. Suppressed REM sleep has been associated with increased irritability and difficulty concentrating the next day. Think of dreams as a good place to work out aggression while you are going through stress at work. You do not want to do away with this valuable release valve.

If you drink coffee on an empty stomach in the morning, a variety of problems will develop. If you skip breakfast your thinking ability will be compromised and emotions will be destabilized. The ill effects of drinking caffeine on an empty stomach will not be apparent immediately. But, approximately one to two hours after consumption you will crash and probably have more difficulty concentrating then had you eaten breakfast. When consuming caffeine on an empty stomach you will be using energy reserves stored in your fat cells, which are typically available during times of severe deprivation such as when fasting or starving. After this compromised spurt in energy, you will be more depleted than before and probably feel free-floating anxiety.

It is important to note that many caffeinated soft drinks have as many as four to five tablespoonfuls of sugar in one can. Therefore, not only do you get the buzz and drop-off from the caffeine, but also the ill effects from the sugar.

If you consume a lot of caffeine and sugar and don't eat three balanced meals a day, this diet will greatly decrease your ability to deal with stress. If you fall into this pattern you may feel that you need more sugar and caffeine.

This is what happened to Tim. During the previous few months, he had felt that he needed an "added boost" to get him through the day. As a title insurance manager he was always particularly stressed during the peak of the home-buying season. This season was no exception. He found that by the end of the day he felt depleted. He had been coming into the office early to deal with the added workload. Often skipping breakfast, he put a pot of coffee in his office. He frequently felt nervous and scattered until 11 a.m. then grabbed a doughnut. For the next 45 minutes, he felt a little better. But then he felt even more nervous and scattered than he did before 11 a.m.

His co-workers found him irritable and pushy. He began to experience diarrhea and restlessness. Then he had a severe bout of insomnia, often coming into work exhausted and sleep deprived. Occasionally, when a clump of new files landed on his desk, he found himself in a full-blown panic attack. Within minutes of feeling the panic he dropped everything and walked outside to catch his breath.

Finally, he went to his primary care physician and asked for what he called "some medication to calm my nerves." Tim was fortunate to have a conscientious and thorough physician who sent him to a psychologist, Dr. Mellow. When Tim told Dr. Mellow that he was "having to drink a pot of coffee a day to keep going," he was surprised that instead of recommending a medication Dr. Mellow asked him to eat three meals a day and not to drink more than two cups of coffee a day.

After going through a two-day withdrawal from caffeine with headaches and fatigue, Tim began to feel that he was better able to concentrate and felt a calm sense of energy. He also found that he was far better able to get work done than just a week ago.

If you have fallen into the same trap as Tim, do what he did to straighten out your diet. Eat three balanced meals a day and minimize sugar and caffeine.

If you are suffering from any major health problems, your body is already compromised. A poor diet will not only make the illness worse but greatly diminish your capacity to cope with a stressful job.

If you are obese or have other health problems, your ability to deal with stress may be compromised. Thus, it is critically important for you to get your health problem under control to be able to function at an optimal level. Not doing so will give you a damaging handicap.

Think of your diet as critical to building a foundation from which you develop good coping skills. Without a balanced diet, whatever coping strategy you develop will fall apart like a house of cards. You are what you eat.

CHAPTER 5

Taking the Edge Off?

DURING THE LAST 25 YEARS there has been an increase of drug and alcohol use in the workplace. It is such a problem that in response to this epidemic many organizations now require random drug testing. In fact, according to one recent study of firms, workplace testing is up 277 percent since 1977. The federal government requires transportation companies to regularly test their drivers, pilots, and captains. Since the passage of the Drug Free Workplace Act in 1988, workplaces that receive federal grants or contracts must be drug free.

Despite all these efforts, many employees who still use mind-altering substances work in non-regulated industries and don't receive a sophisticated degree of scrutiny. This is especially the case if they consume drugs and/or alcohol on the weekends or after work to "relax."

If you are one of these people, it's time to consider a new way of relaxing. You may not know that the effects of drugs and alcohol impair your concentration, memory, and energy level for days after you use these substances. Though you may not be intoxicated on Monday morning, your cognitive abilities are not up to par.

Alcohol and most drugs cause deficits in motivation, optimism, and energy level for several days and even weeks after you last use. If you have these difficulties you probably misread social cues and overreact to social stress. Worse yet, you probably have little insight into the fact that your interpersonal relationships are distorted because of your use.

You may feel that you need "a little something" to unwind or take the edge off after a rough day at work. Maybe you think that you deserve a few indulgences such as alcohol or marijuana because you "have worked hard and now deserve to relax." You may not know the price you pay biologically, psychologically, and socially. But the relief you get from alcohol or marijuana is short-lived. This practice of "taking the edge off" results in a brief period of pleasure when you have the "buzz," but it actually puts the edge back on as much as a week later.

In this chapter, I will describe how alcohol and marijuana will actually complicate your effort to deal with job stress. Not only will you have more difficulty thinking and maintaining emotional stability, but your interpersonal relationships will be at best strained.

Alcohol

There are many myths about the beneficial effects of alcohol. If you accept one or more of these myths as truth, expect multiple problems. Although you believe that alcohol helps you deal with job stress, the fact is it actually contributes to it. Following are some of the main *myths*:

- Alcohol decreases stress.
- Alcohol relieves depression.
- Alcohol decreases anxiety.
- Alcohol is a sleep aid.

The actual *facts* about alcohol are that it causes the following problems as much as several days after you last drank:

- Alcohol increases stress because it lowers the levels of neurotransmitters (that is, GABA) that could help you calm down and deal with stress.
- Alcohol increases anxiety because it lowers GABA. It is quite common for people to have panic attacks precipitated by recent alcohol abuse.
- Alcohol actually increases depression by lowering the levels of the neurotransmitter serotonin for as much as a few weeks after the last drink. Low serotonin causes depression.
- Alcohol destroys deep sleep. It is quite common for people to have alcohol-related insomnia. Alcohol dampens your deep and REM sleep.

There are biopsychosocial consequences to consuming alcohol. The "bio" consequences include deterioration of the body and the brain. The "psych" consequences include deficits in thinking and emotional stability. Finally, the social consequences include difficulties in interpersonal relationships.

Alcohol is toxic to your brain. It *will* kill your brain cells. It lowers blood flow to the brain and impairs your brain chemistry. It degrades the operation of your neurotransmitters.

The degradation of your neurotransmitters causes numerous emotional and thinking problems weeks after your last drink. Many of the neurotransmitters discussed in Chapter 4 get "down-regulated" after consuming alcohol. As noted earlier, for at least two weeks after your last drink the levels of serotonin in your brain will be less available. Low levels of serotonin are correlated with depression.

If you drink a "night cap," you will have a more shallow sleep than you would have otherwise. Alcohol depresses Stage 4 sleep (the deepest sleep), which is when you get the most rest and your immune system is recharged. Alcohol also dampens Rapid Eye Movement (REM) sleep. Therefore, drinking tonight will not only result in losing the opportunity to get some deep sleep, but it will also distort your dreams and may even cause you to wake up in the middle of the night. This mid-sleep cycle awakening occurs because the effects of alcohol begin to wear off and leave you with more anxiety and tension than you had prior to drinking.

Drinking alcohol can result in up to 50 percent of the total daily caloric intake and in the process restrict the normal consumption of macronutrients: fats, carbohydrates, and proteins. In other words, by drinking you suppress your body's ability to make full use of the food you eat.

The alcohol that you drink today may relax you for a few hours, but during the next few days you will be more apt to experience anxiety about your job than if you did not drink at all. This is because the neurotransmitter GABA becomes suppressed as a result of alcohol consumption. I have seen people through the years that have developed an anxiety disorder as a result of their alcohol consumption. The irony is that believed that they were calming themselves down.

Other neurotransmitters are also depressed as a result of alcohol consumption. Dopamine levels decrease, resulting in fewer feelings of pleasure and motivation. Noreprinephrine levels also decrease, resulting in reduced ability to think clearly and poorer memory. Alcohol depresses the neuropeptides, thus depressing the immune system and causing you to be more susceptible to a virus or other illness. Finally, if you are suffering from chronic pain connected to an injury, the intensity of your pain will increase over the long term even though you may feel temporary relief after a drink.

Alcohol damages specific areas of the brain, particularly the hippocampus and the cerebellum. The hippocampus is critically important in the process of learning and laying down of memories. The hippocampus is also the site-specific target for stress hormones. Glucocorticoids (GCs) result in a neurotoxic effect, which weakens the hippocampus. Alcohol activates the hypothalamic-pituitary-adrenal (HPA) axis and elevates GCs, actually initiating the stress response. In other words, though having a drink feels initially like you are "mellowing out," you are actually raising the levels of stress hormones.

From a psychological point of view, alcohol leads to "cognitive constriction," meaning that your capacities to think broadly will wither away and narrow. You will be more prone to black-and-white frames of reference rather than appreciate the shades of gray. You will be more apt to think of bad bosses versus good bosses or the good co-worker versus the co-worker, which will make you less able to deal with the actual complexities of interpersonal experience. Obviously, no one is actually all good or all bad. Alcohol will narrow your focus when you should develop a broad perspective. You need to be mentally flexible, not rigid.

Alcohol also contributes to "affective constriction," meaning that you will feel emotions on the extremes. You will tend to feel either bad or good, not in between. As a result of these extreme emotions, you will feel less emotionally flexible to withstand the changing dynamics in your workplace.

For several years, I taught a seminar in psychological and neuropsychological testing was given to doctoral psychology interns. One of the rules about testing people who have consumed alcohol on a regular basis is that you "do not test a wet brain." This means that people who drink on a regular basis have a variety of deficits in their ability to think, such as:

- Decreased performance on tests of visual and spatial perception.
- Decrease visual and spatial learning ability.
- Decreased ability to make fine motor movements.
- Decreased adaptive abilities.
- Decreased short-term memory.
- Decreased nonverbal abstract learning.
- Decreased abstract thinking ability.
- Decreased conceptual thinking ability.

In addition to these deficits, people who drink on a regular basis develop specific personality characteristics. These traits contribute to greater difficulty trying to get along with co-workers and supervisors. The common characteristics of someone who drinks include:

- Impulsiveness.
- Restlessness.
- Self-centeredness.
- Self-destruction.
- Stubbornness.
- Irritability.
- Ill-humor.
- Arrogance.
- Low self-esteem.
- Procrastination.
- Self-pity.
- Sulkiness.

If you drink regularly and some of these characteristics are familiar, chances are you will be more prone to have interpersonal conflicts with supervisors and co-workers. You may be more prone to be late for work, take more sick days, and perform poorly when you are at work.

If you are like many drinkers, you may have little insight into why you are having all these problems. You may be in a state of denial that it stems from your drinking. Perhaps you argue that you need to "chill out" after dealing with those "toxic" supervisors and co-workers.

This is precisely how Bud deluded himself. For several months he had been feeling that his job had contributed to a great deal of stress since an argument with his boss. The night after this argument he tried to soothe himself with a few beers. He continued to drink each night thereafter, thinking that he was "taking the edge off." His sleep deteriorated; he woke up at approximately 2 a.m. and had trouble getting back to sleep. He continued to drink for the next two months thinking that it relaxed him and helped with sleep. Fred, his co-worker, noticed that he seemed to be more "on edge" than a few months ago. One day Fred approached him and said, "You just don't seem like the same old Bud. What happened?"

Bud responded by telling him about the argument with the supervisor. Fred said that it was "old news" and that the supervisor had "mellowed out."

"Oh no," Bud snapped, "He's the same old jerk he always was. Are you on his side?"

Fred recoiled as if a snake had bitten him and retreated from the room.

When Bud arrived home that night he drank a few more beers than his usual two. He barked at his kids and told his wife that "now the others are out to get me too." Then he drank a few more beers to "cool out."

Bud became increasingly depressed. After a few weeks his family began to avoid him. His brother pulled him aside after Thanksgiving dinner when he noticed that Bud drank several beers. Bud tried to tell him about the job stress and how the family would not let him alone. To Bud's amazement, his brother lent him no sympathy and told him flatly that he noticed a gradual deterioration in his mood and attitude as his drinking increased.

Bud spit back, "What are you calling me, an alcoholic or something? Come on, cut me some slack. I need to relax and get some sleep."

His brother told him about an article he read in a magazine that described how sleep is actually destroyed by drinking and how most people become depressed. His brother asked Bud to quit drinking.

Bud reluctantly quit. He slowly began to feel his old self coming back. After a week his sleep improved, and after two weeks he began to feel more optimistic. Family members began to notice that he was less irritable. At work his co-workers found that his edginess had subsided. Soon thereafter Bud and his supervisor were talking once again.

What would have happened to Bud if his brother did not confront him about his drinking? What would have happened if he disregarded his brother's feedback as meddlesome? Chances are his mood would have deteriorated further. Most of his relationships with family and co-workers would have gotten worse. Bud's job stress may have eventually caused the loss of his job.

Just a Little Toke?

You may be one of those people who feel that you are well served by a few tokes of a joint of marijuana. You may feel that marijuana is what you need to mellow out after a stressful day. If so, it is time to reconsider.

My generation, which came of age during the 1960s, promoted marijuana as a safe and even healthy alternative to the most popular drug of our parents' generation, alcohol. To this day people still argue that it is just an herb. To complicate matters, researchers from my generation hesitated to do serious research on the harmful effects of marijuana.

Just as considerable evidence of marijuana's destructive effects finally did come to light, the "medical marijuana" debate broke out. Soon cancer, glaucoma, and chronic pain patients were seeking a "prescription of marijuana." Medical marijuana initiatives emerged on state ballots.

When I try to explain to patients how marijuana may actually be adding to their job stress, they often counter by asking, "Yeah, sure, then why are doctors prescribing it? Now that I am going through this job stress I may need a prescription too." I explain that some cancer patients are using it to increase their appetite during chemotherapy, or glaucoma patients take it because of the build up in pressure in their eyes, and that job stress is an entirely different matter.

The fact remains that marijuana causes serious difficulties with thinking and emotional stability. Marijuana is notorious for causing short-term memory deficits and difficulty maintaining attention. People who smoke marijuana regularly have a great deal of trouble having clarity of thought. They experience cloudy, confused, and often befuddled thoughts. Their perception regarding their job stress is confounded by irrelevant details and "insights" that are not at all insightful.

It's very common for people who smoke marijuana to become irritable and mildly depressed. They are also prone to lack initiative and motivation. Each of these problems fuel the other. In other words, as you become more depressed, your motivation drops. But because motivation typically decreases for people who use marijuana regularly, it also contributes to depression. This is based on the fact that as you disengage activities that contribute to higher self-esteem, you will in effect feel deflated. In other words, as your motivation drops you gain fewer rewards from your actions, you find few reasons to feel good about yourself, and you become depressed.

The chemical found in marijuana, referred to as THC mimics a chemical in your brain called anandamide. Unlike neurotransmitters that affect brain cells directly, anandamide is a neuromodulator. It orchestrates the activity of several neurotransmitters at the same time. If your brain is flooded with THC, the anandamide effect will temporarily "enhance" (or distort) your perception. This "virtual novelty" may make a simple doorknob seem like the most exquisite doorknob you have ever seen. Unfortunately, you may look at that same doorknob several hours later and wonder what is so special about it.

To make matters worse, because THC creates this rush of anandamide reactions in your brain, many of the neurotransmitters you need to think clearly and feel good aren't as readily available. With less serotonin, GABA, dopamine, and norepinephrine, you will feel more depressed, stressed, have less motivation, and find that your short-term memory is clouded.

Most of this information is quite new, and many people in our society still regard marijuana as a harmless herb. This is the trap Herbert fell into. As an electrician for a large contractor of tract homes, Herb felt increasing stress to wire up a number of houses simultaneously. Since his apprenticeship program, he had periodically used marijuana with friends. But now with an overwhelming amount of job stress he decided he needed a way to "check out for awhile." He asked a friend to arrange a purchase of an ounce of marijuana.

After the kids were asleep, he stepped out into the garage to smoke until he felt "set for the evening." Despite his wife's criticism, this became a nightly ritual. He felt the troubles of the day melt away as he "mellowed out." However, soon his wife complained that he had become remote and moody. He responded by saying that he was "unwinding and trying to work things out in my head."

Yet Herb actually spent considerable time muddled in thought. Soon he found that he was less able to concentrate at work. On one occasion he made a serious error resulting in having to rewire an entire house, which held up the carpenters. When the general contractor pulled Herb aside and asked why he had been so slow lately, Herb did not know what to say. He knew that he was feeling particularly sluggish and felt much less motivated than he had just a few months ago. When he tried to think about his situation, his thoughts were cloudy. But he did remember that there was one change from a few months ago: He now smoked marijuana on a regular basis. He decided to quit just to see if his concentration would improve. Although in the first week he felt no change, he slowly began to feel less muddled and was thinking more clearly. Gradually his energy and enthusiasm returned.

Smoking marijuana is not a reasonable coping strategy for job stress. If you smoke, quit. A word of caution, however: THC is stored in your fat cells and will take weeks to leech out. Thus, you will not experience relief from the symptoms of quitting until weeks after quitting. Some people make the mistake of saying to themselves, "Well, I quit and I still have the same problems, so I might as well go back to smoking." You need to give yourself the time your entire body needs to cleanse itself of THC. Once cleansed, you can go on to develop some of the coping strategies outlined in the rest of the book.

CHAPTER 6

Harassment

IF YOU HAVE BEEN HARASSED or discriminated against, there are psychological and legal remedies that you can employ to protect yourself.

If you think that you have been harassed because of your race, age, or sex, there are government agencies you should know about. The Employment Equal Opportunity Commission (EEOC) investigates cases of discrimination including but not limited to race and age. The Labor Commission oversees labor law and insures that union-staffed employers abide by basic labor standards.

These two government agencies are your resources. If you feel you have been discriminated against or that your company is not following basic labor laws, call for consultation. Your call may result in an investigation.

There are several types of harassment. The two most common types include sexual harassment and general harassment. Both can be emotionally debilitating. In this chapter, you will learn how to deal with both types.

Sexual Harassment

In 1964, sexual harassment was deemed illegal by the federal government under Title VII as a form of discrimination. Despite this law, many women didn't feel comfortable telling anyone about being sexually harassed until recently. Sexual harassment in the workplace didn't completely garner the public attention until the Senate confirmation hearings of Supreme Court nominee Clarence Thomas. Anita Hill described how she had endured Mr. Thomas's constant sexual advances and lewd comments. Although Thomas was eventually confirmed to sit on the Supreme Court, thousands of women felt that the social conditions had changed enough to file a grievance or a suit based on sexual harassment.

There are two general types of sexual harassment. The first and the easiest to recognize is referred to as the "quid pro quo," or "you do something for me and I will do something for you." In this case the harasser says to the victim, "You have sex with me and I will…promote you, give you a raise, or insure your transfer."

The second type is the most contested and controversial form of harassment. It involves a sexually charged or hostile environment. This can involve anything from lewd comments made by co-workers to graffiti, nude pictures pinned on office walls, or sexual advances made by co-workers.

The issue of sexual harassment centers on the question of whether or not the attention is unwelcome and repeated. If you ask the perpetrator to stop and he doesn't, then you can more easily make a case that he is harassing you.

There are several critical questions you should ask yourself if you are wondering whether you have been sexually harassed. Following is a checklist of pertinent questions:

- Was the flirtation reciprocal?
- Did you give any indication that you were open to that type of attention?
- Had you yourself made comments about how he or she looked?

If you answered yes to any of these questions, it may complicate your case. Your employer will argue that you invited the attention. Further, if you attempt to file a grievance or pursue a legal case, your employer may argue that you have become disgruntled over a romantic relationship gone sour.

Harassment is *unwelcome,* while mutual flirtation indicates openness. Some mild forms of flirtation are complimentary, while harassment always feels bad. Flirtation is reciprocal and equal, whereas harassment is one-sided and about power.

Given that adults may spend the majority of their waking weekday time at work, the workplace serves as one of the chief sources of social contact. It is quite common that some men and women meet and begin relationships at work. Often these relationships begin with one person somehow indicating that he is interested in going beyond a collegial relationship. But after the overture is made and you have not responded with mutual interest, he should back off. If he does not back off, he may have sexually harassed you.

Many people don't complain of sexual harassment in the workplace because they think:

1. "I will be embarrassed," or "If I complain everyone will think I am a whiner," or "I won't be able to look anyone in the eye."
2. "If I complain they will get back at me," or "Maybe I'll loose my job over it."
3. "What is the use," or "Nobody will do anything."

All of these reasons for not making a report are self-defeating rationalizations. They reflect a sense of helplessness. Although it is true that in the past complaining about sexual harassment was met with ridicule or actual sexual assault, now harassment is illegal.

Before pursuing a legal case or grievance, make sure that you make your displeasure known. If you are uncomfortable with the attention, tell the other person. Make sure that your displeasure is voiced clearly and there is no question that you don't want to pursue a relationship. If the other person does not stop, go to his supervisor. Make sure that you follow the company policy if you pursue the matter further. Clearly document the incidents of harassment. If you give your notes to a supervisor, retain a copy.

Most companies and organizations have a written policy concerning sexual harassment. Ask your supervisor to show you the company's policy. All managers should possess a copy and be thoroughly familiar with the policy. When I was the Chief Psychologist at Kaiser Permanente Medical Center in Vallejo, California, I was required to read its policy on sexual harassment. I kept it on hand for reference if one of the staff psychologists asked questions about it or made a report claiming to have been sexually harassed by a co-worker.

Hopefully you are not convinced that reporting incidents of sexual harassment will result in more harassment. If you have endured sexual harassment you may believe that the laws against harassment are too weak to protect you.

This was the rationalization made by Patricia. She worked for 10 years as an administrative assistant to the vice president of Domp Chemical Company. They enjoyed a relationship of mutual respect. But after he retired, she was reassigned to a new vice president and everything changed. Soon after they began working together he made several comments about her appearance. Initially, he said, "You are looking great! You must have had a great weekend." Then he shifted to, "How do you keep your body so fit?" A week later he said, "Looking sexy today!" Patricia had felt complemented until that last comment.

Instead of thanking him as she had for the previous comments she said nothing, fearing that he would think of her as "too sensitive." Then one day she stooped down to pick up a paper and he leered at her saying, "Oh Trish, I'll have to drop paper more often."

Patricia felt so embarrassed and offended that she rushed out of the office. But later that afternoon he called her back into his office to take notes while he talked to a client on the speaker phone. As the phone call wore on he seemed less interested in the conversation and more in watching her take notes.

He stood up and walked behind her, peering over her should. Leaning down over her shoulder, he pointed at a line she had written. But as he lifted his arm it grazed her breast.

She recoiled, standing abruptly.

"Excuse me," he said.

She sat back down. The conference continued with the client at the other end oblivious to the fact that the vice president was very distracted.

After he hung up, he said, "Well Trish, why don't you type that up and we'll go over it. Say at dinner?"

"Oh, ah...." she found herself stammering. "I've got some plans tonight."

"Okay," he said unfazed. "Bring it in tomorrow morning."

After work that evening, she called her friend Brenda and told her all about the incident. Brenda told her to make a report.

"No, I can't do that!" Patricia replied. "I'll be shifted back to the secretarial pool. I've worked too hard to get to where I am."

"But you've got rights," Brenda protested.

"Not in my company. It's a good old boys club."

The next morning she reported to the vice president as requested. He looked up from the notes she had typed and said, "Well you do real nice work Trish. You can go far in this company. I could see to it that things happen for you."

Though Patricia was still quite leery of him, she responded, "Oh thanks. It is true that I hoped to crash the glass ceiling here."

"Stick with me and you will. Now how about that dinner? Maybe tonight?"

"Oh, I'm sorry I've got plans again."

He looking mildly disappointed said, "Looks like you're a popular girl. Any guy I know?"

"No, it's not like that," she responded, knowing immediately that she should have said that there was someone else.

"Good."

That night she called Brenda again.

"You've got to stop it before it goes too far."

She realized that Brenda was right. The next morning when she delivered some papers to him she said, "Remember yesterday when I said there wasn't anyone. Well there is." She felt relieved, thinking he would back off.

Instead, he walked up and placed his palm on her cheek and said, "Well, he doesn't have to know anything, does he?"

She abruptly left the office, walking past her desk and straight to the human resources department. She asked to see a copy of the company policy on sexual harassment. Relieved to see that there was a policy, she made a copy and made copious notes over the next hour.

Based on what she read in the policy, she decided to return to the vice president's office to make a clear statement that she was not open to his advances. But he said, "Oh Trish, what are you going to do. Come on! You know you want it as bad as I do."

She responded by saying, "You leave me with no choice." Then she left the office knowing that there was no more she needed to say.

She filed a grievance with the human resources department as specified in the policy. When the company failed to respond with a transfer to a parallel position, she hired an attorney. Only after a suit was filed did her company make an accommodation for her.

Patricia was wise to review the company policy. She needed to demonstrate that she used all the remedies offered by the company before she could call a halt to her boss's behavior. Finding that he continued the harassment after she made a clear statement, she was able to take it to the next level: a grievance. When the company balked at her request for a transfer, she took it to the next level: a suit. At that point lawyers representing the company knew they had no recourse but to accommodate her.

Many organizations have reacted to charges of sexual harassment by requiring that their employees attend a training seminar on the subject. The presentations usually begin by describing the changes in the social climate of the workplace, noting that in the not-too-distant past people used to make sexual comments and not be held accountable. Today, however, that type of behavior can be subject to disciplinary action against the perpetrator and a lawsuit by the victim.

Do not allow yourself to be subjected to sexual harassment. Use your company's policy and the legal system to protect yourself.

The Tyrant

Unfortunately, some supervisors want a supervisory position because of the power and status that comes with the job. If these managers do not feel that they have experienced respect and acclaim in their new position, they may try to squeeze it out of those they supervise. When they feel that their workers have not shown enough respect, they may regard those workers as insubordinate.

Some supervisors bully those working for them. If your supervisor is one of these people and he knows that he can "get your goat," he will probably continue to abuse his power. You must therefore act as if you have thick skin and let his comments roll off of you without sticking. If they strike and you act wounded, you may receive more of the same treatment. Bullies attack those people who are vulnerable. If you react to a bully by appearing vulnerable, he will act like he is a shark that has seen blood.

So what are workers to do if they are in a subordinate position to a supervisor who is a bully? How can you survive a supervisor who has not so blatantly harassed you that you can file a claim with the EEOC or the Labor Commission?

Milfred found himself in this middle ground. He worked as an insurance application processor and felt that he was the prime target of his unit supervisor. Whenever his supervisor was in a bad mood he seemed to pick on Wilfred. Wilfred usually responded by looking rattled and asking his supervisor if he could process extra applications. His supervisor typically responded by saying, "Yeah, sure. If you can handle it."

After his supervisor left the room his co-workers would shake their heads and look at Milfred with pity. One of them finally asked him, "Why do you let him get away with that?" Milfred looked befuddled. "Why doesn't he bother you?" His co-worker went on saying, "We just ignore him."

Milfred tried this approach, but it did not work right away. His supervisor was so used to Milfred's subservient response that he continued to harass him for a few weeks. But Milfred held his ground. After the second week he was relieved to find that his supervisor found another target for his aggression.

If you are experiencing the same type of abuse as Milfred, do not wait for a co-worker's encouragement to change your behavior. Make sure that you do not provide a target for a bully.

One way to protect yourself from harassment is to step out of the line of fire. If you cannot withdraw, then allow the offending person's assault to backfire without standing in the way. You need to be able to practice interpersonal judo. In other words, you can step aside and allow your supervisor to trip on his own assault. He will not suffer the consequences of his own actions unless you react differently. For example, if your supervisor says something to you that borders on verbal abuse but would not by itself hold up in court, politely and with a straight face ask him to repeat it as if you had not heard his comment. This technique is especially effective if there are witnesses. In such situations your supervisor may be compelled to reflect on the tone and flavor of the comment.

Audrey learned to use interpersonal judo to deal with an abusive co-worker turned supervisor. She was able to tolerate Katherine's subtle verbal abuse when they were both accounting clerks. But after Katherine's promotion their relationship changed for the worse. Katherine made an effort to demonstrate her authority by making rude comments usually directed at Audrey. After the last audit she turned to Audrey and said, "Well it appears that if it wasn't for you we could have finished this job a long time ago." Audrey looked at her co-workers and saw their eyebrows raised. She decided that she needed to call an end to this abuse. Then she turned to Katherine, careful not to sound defensive, and said, "I'm sorry Katherine, I didn't hear what you said. What did you say?"

Katherine took the bait. "I said that you seem to be dragging all of us down."

Audrey looked all around and saw that all her co-workers had heard the comment. They looked at Katherine with their mouths hanging open. Katherine immediately understood that she had made a major blunder. She turned and rushed out of the office.

Audrey knew she had enough to file a grievance. She had carefully kept copies of her notes from previous incidents. Now she knew she had the witnesses she needed.

By using interpersonal judo, Audrey not only deflected a vicious attack but she may have changed the dynamics in the office to such an extent that Katherine will think twice before making another rude comment. By insuring that there were witnesses, Audrey showed Katherine that everyone would be watching for a further outbreak of rudeness. If Katherine is like most people, she will try to "prove" that she is not rude by being overly polite.

Very few of us can tolerate bullies and bossy co-workers. You cannot always manage to stay away from them. Nor is it a useful strategy to passively accept their manipulation, as illustrated by Milfred's experience. Fighting force with force escalates the tension. With conversational judo, don't try to resist their bossiness. Instead, step aside so that the tone of their voice or the unreasonableness of their request looks obvious to them. If they say, "Do it this way," but you know that their way doesn't work, say, "I'm not sure I understand; could you show me?" When they fail to show that their way works, resist the temptation to rub it in. Their failure will stand on its own.

The bottom line is that no one should tolerate harassment. If you are plagued by harassment, make sure that you explore your options. You may be able to use some of the intermediate steps described here to deflect the abuse. If this is not possible, then you must use the system in place to protect yourself legally. Either way, you have more power than you think.

CHAPTER 7

Human Conflict in the Workplace

MUCH HUMAN COMMUNICATION IS BASED on misunderstanding. Many of these misunderstandings occur at work and are especially pronounced during periods when we are stressed. Work can present itself as a pressure cooker for social conflict.

In this chapter, I will focus on how you can avoid becoming entangled in the quagmire of interpersonal conflict in the workplace.

Those "Other" People

We all have to deal with difficult people at work. Given the variety of personalities you undoubtedly will find someone who is irritating. Therefore, you will need to be observant, flexible, and adaptable to the changing social circumstances in your workplace.

Few workplaces are without office politics. Gossip is one of the most seductive aspects of office politics and is often the basis for conflict. But, the more you participate in gossip, the greater the chance that you will be the target of it.

So how do you extract yourself from the tangled web of factional disputes? First of all, you must stop stoking the flames by participating in the divisions. You may think you are an innocent bystander. But if you stop to think for a moment, it will probably become evident that you are not totally innocent of participation.

If this is the case, making some kind of verbal request for a truce would help. A meeting between you and key figures in the opposing group will provide the cover you need to demonstrate good faith. If you are represented by a union, make sure that a union representative is present. By stating on record that you want no part of the conflict, you will provide yourself with insulation from further criticism for being involved in partisan disputes.

When dealing with workplace conflict, you will need to take a step back to examine how you are responding differently to each individual. Some individuals require a great degree of finesse to deal with effectively.

For example, passive dependent people may get under your skin because they rely on you to solve their problems. Try not to fall in the trap of doing things for them that they can do for themselves. Whenever possible, use your interpersonal judo skills to turn their request for help into encouragement for them to be self-sufficient. Praise them for their success as they attempt to accomplish the task that they had asked you to perform. Do not jump in and help them finish the task because you know that you are more skillful.

Debra learned the wisdom of this approach only after a period of frustration. She and Marta had worked together for 10 years as clerks in a wholesale pluming supply company. Although their duties have remained the same, Debra had grown to be frustrated with Marta's manipulations. She began to feel that her relationship with Marta was extremely draining. She found herself trying to avoid Marta. Each time a new assignment came in, Marta said, "Oh, could you help me?"

Debra frequently fell into the trap of helping Marta. Within a very short period of time she found herself doing the majority of the work. Debra was extremely frustrated and resentful; she was determined not to perform the task for her. She decided to try a new approach. When Marta asked again for help, Debra responded by saying, "I'll help you learn."

Debra was careful not to jump in and finish the task. She stood back, giving Marta suggestions. Despite Marta's frequent attempts to enlist her in the actual work, Debra held her ground. When Marta finally did complete the task, Debra gave her warm praise.

But soon the boss asked Marta again to fill another order of the same kind. Marta turned to Debra asking for help. Debra referred back to Marta's success, saying, "Oh don't you remember how well you did it before? You don't need my help." But then Marta responded by saying, "Yes, but you do such a better job than I." Debra smiled, "I've had more practice and I don't want to stand in the way of *you* getting practice."

Debra's technique was tactful and clear. Had she simply said no, she may have felt guilty for being rude. Because she made the point that she would only act as adviser, Marta relied on herself.

Some people like Martha are dependent and aggressive at the same time. They are usually described as "passive-aggressive." They have an uncanny ability to set up circumstances whereby they do not have to follow through on a task, and you may find yourself completing it for them. But even after you do it for them, they still may complain that it was not good enough. They may conveniently disappear when it is time to clean up. Alternatively, they may do such a poor job that either you do it yourself or your supervisor delegates it to you to insure that it is done properly.

Set limits with a passive-aggressive person. Your task will be to keep her assignment in her court. If she tries to avoid picking out an assignment, insure that your assignment is clear with your supervisor. If your task is Part A and your co-worker's is Part B, complete only A, even if you fear that she will do a poor job on Part B.

If you work with someone who monopolizes conversations or seems to always have an ax to grind, you will need to make clear that your ears have limits. Ask him to get to the point. If the same point is made several times, remind him of that fact. If he senses a little irritation in your voice, it is not the end of the world. In effect, you will have emphasized the fact that you are not receptive to endless monologues and negative tirades. He will look for other ears to listen.

When dealing with the interpersonal conflicts of the workplace you can be passive, aggressive, or assertive. If you respond to other people passively, you will invite manipulation and abuse. You will be holding up a sign that reads, "It's okay to treat me badly because I don't respond." If you are overly passive and play the "possum defense" you may hope that the attacker becomes bored and walks away. You may say, "I don't like to make waves." Yet the waves come your way anyway.

Take Mildred for example. Her secretarial pool had been in chaos ever since the downsizing of her company. Virtually all of her co-workers were on edge. It seemed to Mildred that she needed to make sure that there were no more waves than there already were tumbling through the pool. Consequently, Mildred accepted a larger workload than anyone else because she thought it would be easier to do the work than upset any of her co-workers. Mildred became increasingly stressed but kept this fact to herself. Soon she began to lose sleep and plunged into a depression.

Soon her co-workers were venting their frustrations on her. She found them to be cranky and unwilling to make changes. She decided that she would compensate by taking on still more work.

She realized that there was a severe cost to her passive and co-dependent behavior. The waves that she was trying to prevent were actually greater for her than her co-workers. It finally dawned on her that setting limits and saying no to extra work cost her less energy than simply doing more than her fair share. "Besides," she thought, "they are going to be cranky no matter what I do."

By not compensating for her co-workers passive-aggressive behavior Mildred was able to refocus her attention on how she was adjusting to the changes in the company. Mildred managed to cope with the changes by transforming her passivity into taking care of herself.

The solution to passivity is not just to go to the other extreme. Unfortunately, people are often told to "stand up for yourself and get into their faces." Aggression actually results in more stress for everyone, and it does not always result in getting your way. Aggressive people are avoided, disliked, and criticized behind their backs. Because they perpetually appear self-righteous, entitled, and self-centered, they push people away.

This is what happened to Bertha. When the news of downsizing came, she responded in a completely opposite way than did Mildred. Bertha let everyone know she was not going to do any extra work; if anyone wanted any help, she told them to "look for some other patsy, like Mildred." Bertha would tap her foot at the copy machine if she had to wait behind one of her co-workers. When the supervisor asked her secretarial pool to rush a typed report she responded by saying, "Forget it! Not me."

Her co-workers began to avoid her during breaks and lunch. No longer was she invited to the dinner parties. Bertha lost what social support system she had left and did not know what hit her.

Then she began to wonder why she had become socially isolated. She asked Diane, one of her co-workers. "I feel like you all think I have leprosy. No one wants to have me around."

"What do you expect. You're nasty all the time," Diane responded, surprising both of them by her bluntness.

Bertha realized that she was pushing people away. Although she was angry with management for making the decision to downsize, she had no beef with her co-workers. She decided to apologize for her behavior. Within a few weeks she began to enjoy social contact with her co-workers once again.

Had Diane not revealed the reason why Bertha was being avoided, little would have changed. Bertha probably would have vented her anger on her co-workers and blindly wondered why she was so socially isolated. Even after Diane confronted her, Bertha may not have apologized for her rude behavior. By swallowing her pride and facing the fact that her co-workers did not deserve to be the target of her misdirected anger, she slowly regained the friendships of her co-workers.

In contrast to both the passive and aggressive interpersonal styles, the assertive style is a way of standing up for yourself without "getting into anyone's face." Assertive people make their opinions known but they do it in such a way that it does not violate one anyone's rights. Assertive people know where they stand but they also respect the opinions of others. As a result, they gain the respect of others while they advance toward their own goals.

Diane managed to avoid both Mildred's and Bertha's mistakes. During the downsizing she refused to respond with either passivity or aggression. She decided that she was going to do her fair share of the work; nothing more, nothing less. She told the others, "We are going to divide the work evenly." When Bertha said, "I won't do it," Diane responded, "That is your option. But we will still divide the work up and each of us will know what our assignment is." Though Diane suffered from the stress of an increased workload, like her co-workers, she knew quite well that by insisting on clarity in assignments she would not suffer from the more severe problems such as those experienced by Mildred and Bertha.

By avoiding the passive extreme of Mildred's behavior and the aggressive extreme of Bertha's attitude, she was able to deal with the stress of downsizing without creating more stress for herself. From this point of view, we could say that being assertive is the most "economical" manner in which to conduct yourself during periods of change in your company. By being assertive people will know where you stand, what your limits are, and you will only work your fair share.

Social Shock Absorbers

If you take every incident, every interaction with co-workers and supervisors, as weighty and of the utmost importance, your stress level will be needlessly overloaded. Our communication with co-workers and supervisors are laced with potential misunderstandings. Everyone has his own point of view and is "right" from his perspective. If you do not allow yourself a little slack, each misunderstanding will result in unnecessary tension.

The workplace is a bumpy social road that you must travel each day. You need to insure that you have "social shock absorbers" to be able to travel this bumpy road. You will need to be both flexible when dealing with your peers and adaptable to changing conditions. Flexibility and adaptability will provide the shock absorbers that you will need so that you will not break an axle or become overly stressed.

You need internal as well as external shock absorbers whereby each event is cushioned or buffered in your mind. You will need to learn to take things less seriously, to lighten up and develop flexibility if you expect to avoid job stress.

If you expect to survive the complex social group of the workplace emotionally unscathed you will need to develop flexibility. This flexibility is not unlike having shock absorbers when dealing with people at work. Given there will always be people who will clash with your personality, having shock absorbers will allow you the flexibility necessary to continue to work without being brutalized by conflict.

If you expect that there will periodically be misunderstandings inherent between you and various people at work, then when they do occur you will be better able to take them in stride. On the other hand, if you expect that people at work will see things the way that you do, you are setting yourself up for frequent rude awakenings. If you find yourself disturbed by the fact that someone at work cannot understand your position, do not lock yourself into the expectation that he must. By locking into your position, you are really setting a course for confrontation with your co-workers. Then, if during the confrontation you develop a self-righteous attitude that the other person adopt your position, you will set yourself up for a no-win situation. Self-righteous inflexibility actually incites conflict, similar in many ways to a red cape in a bullfight.

If your co-workers feel that you are arrogant, they probably won't be receptive to your ideas or feedback; arrogant people are usually defended against. When they express an opinion, typically people pay closer attention to how that opinion is expressed than the ideas it contains.

Red found himself in this self-defeating trap. He had been feeling that many of his co-workers did not appreciate him. As one of six computer technicians, he had developed what he thought of as an efficient way to troubleshoot computer problems in the insurance company. He touted his method as the way that his peers should operate.

Peter told him one day, "We all have our own way of going about our business."

Red retorted, "Yeah, but have you considered that you have been wasting time?"

Peter and the others began to avoid Red. Then the director called Red into his office and asked him if he would be interested in a transfer. When Red declined, the director asked if he was happy in his current position. Red responded by saying, "Yes, but it looks like the guys I'm working with don't seem to appreciate any suggestions."

The director said, "It appears that they are doing fine." Then he told Red that he had another meeting and excused himself.

Red was confused. He wondered why the director asked him if he was happy in his current position. He hadn't told anyone that he was unhappy.

Red reflected on his relationship with his co-workers. He realized that although he had been trying to share his method with his co-workers, the way that he communicated seemed to be more of an issue with everyone then the content of what he was saying. He decided to approach Peter again and apologize for communicating his ideas in an arrogant fashion. To Red's relief, Peter responded by immediately becoming friendly toward him. Soon all of Red's peers became more approachable. In fact, one asked him about his method of troubleshooting.

Red's insight and newfound humility won him the non-skeptical ears of his co-workers. They no longer tuned him out because of his arrogant style. Now the content of his message earned greater attention than did the manner in which he presented it.

If part of your job stress is the result of a series of unfortunate conflicts to which you have contributed, you may want to look clearly at the quilt you have sewn together. You cannot do anything about what the other person has done, but you can acknowledge your part of the conflict. An apology is taking the high road. From the high road, you will be better able to position yourself to be above conflict and insulate yourself from further conflict.

If you have been criticized and are not sure how to respond, take a step back to reflect. It is wise not to respond by either extreme, either by dismissing criticism or feeling devastated by it. A balanced and reflective perspective is critical. There are a number of questions you may want to ask yourself:

1. Have you heard the same criticism from independent sources?
2. Is there any truth in the criticism?
3. Does the criticism have to do with an important part of my life or is it just a hurtful side issue?
4. Was the person simply venting or overdefending himself from something I said?

By asking yourself these questions, you will be better able to communicate to your co-workers without tripping yourself up with self-deluding misunderstandings. If you interact with your co-workers with clarity and demonstrate insight into your own behavior, you will minimize the chances that your job stress is the result of your own actions.

Unraveling "Them"

When feeling stressed at work, it is very easy to feel that you have little support. The surge of anxiety or depression can set you up to be hypersensitive and easily bruised by others. Just as if you had a bruised elbow from a bump into a wall, each little bump would hurt. So, too, when stressed, you "bump into" a misunderstanding with a co-worker or a supervisor; what would have been taken in stride during periods without stress becomes a major source of added stress. If you continue to bump into the same misunderstanding with the same people, you may run the risk of stringing together these experiences and assuming that you see evidence of ill intent. In such a case, you may develop the belief that "they" meant to hurt you.

One of the biggest perceptual mistakes that I have consistently seen is that people experiencing job stress refer to everyone at work as "they." Those people who blame "them" often say, "they did... to me," or "If it wasn't for them I'd...." If you feel that 'they' are all against you it is extraordinarily difficult to cope with job stress.

Through my work of helping people to disentangle "them," we find that there really is no "them." As I help a person identify who "they" are, it turns out that "they" are not a homogeneous group. In other words, each of "they" usually has his or her own perspective. By disentangling "them," we find that people who were assumed to have been part of some sinister alliance do not really participate in any coherent way with the rest of "them." Proceeding further, we find that the rest of "them" do not exist either. The process is much like opening Chinese boxes. Each time you open one box, or in this case identify one person assumed to be part of "them," we find that there is a smaller box yet to open, that the sinister person is not part of "them," and the victim must look elsewhere to identify "them."

If you feel that your job stress is the result of "them," you are like Don Quixote, doing battle with enemies in your own mind. Parry fell into this very trap. For months he felt at odds with his co-workers. Since the management ordered a reorganization of the packinghouse, Parry had been feeling that the management didn't understand the needs of the warehousemen because the plan meant needless work. Parry found it disturbing that his co-workers Bill, Bob, and Ben went along with the plan without a fuss.

Then, when they did nothing to come to his defense when he objected to the plan during a meeting, he began to feel like they were setting him up to be a scapegoat. When he showed up for work in the morning, he found them less friendly toward him than they had been prior to the reorganization. Members of the management also seemed cool toward him.

Parry began to feel that "they" were all conspiring together. He felt anxious when at work, and at home he found himself slump into a depression. His wife asked him why he was so sullen. He responded by saying, "They are all trying to get rid of me. They came up with this plan that they knew I would not go along with."

His wife asked who they were and why he thought that they all agreed that he should be set up. He responded by saying that they are all going along with the plan. She suggested that Bill, Bob, and Ben may be going along with the plan for their own reasons, which may have little to do with him.

He countered by asking, "Then why are they avoiding me?"

She responded, "Maybe your opposition to the plan makes them feel uncomfortable and they are worried that management will get them." She went on to suggest that he talk to his co-workers.

The next day Parry approached Bob and asked him what he thought of the plan. Bob responded by saying, "It stinks!"

Parry was exasperated, "Then why didn't you say anything when I objected during the meeting?"

Bob responded, "I wanted to but I've been written up and I didn't want to draw anymore fire. Look, I've got a wife and kid at home and I need this job."

Later that day Parry approached Bill and asked him the same question. Bill also said that he disagreed with the plan but was now under consideration for a management position himself and wanted to save his objection to the plan until after the selection process was over.

The next morning Parry approached Ben, who told him that he was going through a divorce and feeling too overwhelmed to deal with his feelings about the plan. He added, "Look, I'm just trying to get through the day. That stupid plan is the furthest thing from my mind."

After finding out that his friends were not conspiring against him Parry reinvested his energy into writing up a counterproposal to the plan. He was careful to demonstrate the cost savings in his plan by showing that fewer man-hours would be needed. To his surprise, management was delighted with his initiative and agreed to give it serious consideration.

Had Parry continued to fight "them," he would have stoked up his own paranoia that he had been "stabbed in the back." But because he made the effort to deconstruct the belief that they were in a conspiracy, he freed himself up to focus on orchestrating his energies toward a constructive resolution. Thus, instead of caving in on himself and constructing a mirage of them, he pulled himself together and rechanneled his frustration to develop a constructive plan.

If you are plagued by the concern that they are making it difficult for you at work, take the step back to unravel who "they" are. By making this effort, you will save yourself from being needlessly overwhelmed.

Gossip

Gossip has always been a major source of conflict in the workplace. If you have been the source of gossip, do not confront those gossiping with indignation. An angry confrontation can only result in more gossip. For example, you may make the mistake of walking up to one of the people you had heard was talking negatively about you and say, "I heard you were talking about me. Do you want to say it to my face. Or are you too much of a coward for that!" More than likely they will deny it. Yet after you leave they will gossip about your defensiveness.

Gossiping about those who gossip about you will only make things worse. In other words, if you can talk about the same people behind their backs, eventually they will hear about your gossip and intensify the tension between you.

You can change the dynamics of gossip by thinking nondefensively and responding to people who gossip about you with far more finesse. For example, "Hi, Beth. A few people told me that you had been talking about me. I told them that I was sure you wouldn't do anything like that—I am right, aren't I?" Then punctuate the comment with a friendly non-sarcastic smile.

What can Beth say? You are not only leaving her with the question of who might be talking to you, but you are letting her know that you know about what has been said. You are also putting her on notice that you will hear about future comments. It is probable that Beth will watch what she says in the future.

CHAPTER 8

Seeing Red

WE ALL FEEL ANGRY PERIODICALLY throughout our lives. It is not uncommon to feel angry at work, especially if you are experiencing job stress. Anger is especially stirred up if you think that you have been treated poorly. Thus, because anger is a fact of life, your challenge is to deal with anger effectively. You have a choice between expressing your anger spontaneously without censorship or channeling that anger into constructive behaviors that may result in a resolution to your problems. You can shoot yourself in the foot or you can use your anger as fuel to propel you out of the problems.

If you are one of those people who feel intense anger at your boss or co-workers, it is time to take a step back to reflect. It is difficult to step back when you are seeing red, but you do not want to make more problems for yourself than already exist.

It is not uncommon to encounter co-workers and supervisors who are stewing in anger. Sometimes this anger spills out onto everyone in the workplace. Too often, we have heard of people becoming violent and going on a rampage.

In this chapter, I will focus on how you can deal with your anger and angry co-workers. Because there are a variety of ways people experience and express anger, there are a variety of techniques that you can use to either deal with an angry person or manage your own anger. The most extreme expression of anger is violence.

Losing Control

Losing control has become an all-too-common occurrence, with a disgruntled employee coming into work seeking lethal revenge. Many of the early press reports of murders in the workplace involved post office workers, but lethal force is not restricted to violence among postal employees. Murder in the workplace is rapidly becoming one of the fastest growing types of violence. In the four years between 1989 and 1993, workplace violence tripled. Homicide has since become the second leading cause of death at work.

It has become startlingly common to hear about a man who returned to work with automatic weapons blazing. After such an incident, the shooter's co-workers are usually interviewed by the press. It is common to hear some of those co-workers say, "Well, he kind of kept to himself, but I never had any idea he would do this."

Usually these assassins are walking time bombs. Often, when they return to work, they looking for people who they feel have wronged them. When an Atlanta day trader returned to the stock brokerage, he hunted down people who loaned him money that he lost in day trading. When Dan White returned to the San Francisco City Hall and shot Mayor Moscone and fellow supervisor Harvey Milk, he was convinced they had done him wrong. These assassins feel that there are no options available and the ultimate revenge is the only way to express themselves.

When dealing with an angry person at work and there is no escape, try to lighten the tone of your interaction. One method of doing this is to sit down, if both of you are standing. Speak more slowly than his pressured tirade. By the tone, pace, and inflection of your voice he will unconsciously match yours. This is also the case with the rate of your breathing. By an exaggerated slowing of your breath with deep inhaling and exhaling, he will match you in kind.

Promoting less defensive body language will be matched on his part. Try not to make any gestures that are obviously a put down. Do not, for example, point at him, roll your eyes, or shake your head.

If you are stuck in a break room together and have water or tea available, offer him a glass. The offering will set up a situation in which he will feel compelled to respond by being less confrontational. It will be less likely that he will be prone to violence if you are showing generosity.

If you are wondering about whether or not your co-worker is capable of "violence," consider the following characteristics:

- Many are considered "loners."
- Two thirds were single divorced males in their 30s.
- Alcohol played a minor role.
- Most communicated their intentions prior to the act.
- Many are "gun nuts" or have a "warrior mentality." For example, they own guns and like to dress in camouflage fatigues.
- Most are Caucasian.
- Almost half have a history of violence.
- Many have a history of interpersonal problems and have problems with anger.
- About half are suicidal. After the incident they will either try to get killed or not try to escape.
- Many experienced a significant loss during the year of the incident.
- Many had psychological problems that were evident before the incident.

If you are reading this book, you may not be capable of such angry tirades. But, whether you are seething with anger yourself or trying to stay away from someone who is a walking time bomb, the following section will outline some of the most important ways of dealing with anger.

Neutralizing Anger

There are several misconceptions about anger. These misconceptions serve as rationalizations for expressing anger spontaneously and with no constraints despite the consequences.

In their book, *When Anger Hurts,* Mathew McKay, Peter Rogers, and Judith McKay point out that many people set themselves up to miscommunicate their anger because of embracing four myths:

1. Anger is controlled by uncontrollable physical forces. It is true that anger has been correlated with high levels of prolactin in women, testosterone in men, and high levels of adrenaline and norepinephrine in all people. But it

does *not* follow that we are predisposed biochemically to express our anger uncontrollably.

2. Anger is an instinct. The fact is that we do *not* have a "violent brain" that compels us to aggression. It is true that the expression of anger served an important function in our evolutionary past. When a predator tried to attack, anger mobilized an individual into the fight part of the fight-or-flight response. However, learning to live with other people meant that we needed a larger range of options than just fight-or-flight. With our expanded brain capacity (for example, our frontal lobes), we developed the ability to inhibit impulses of anger.

3. Frustration leads to anger. Unfortunately, many people assume that there are a chain of events that look something like this:

Frustration

Anger

Aggression

But frustration does not necessarily lead to anger. There are numerous emotional and behavioral routes through which we channel frustrated feelings.

4. It is healthy to ventilate anger. There are consequences to aggression. If you yell and lash out at people, you will be the focal point of criticism or legal consequences. No longer will the attention be on what you were angry about. Now the attention will be on the manner in which you expressed yourself.

Though anger is a fact of life, the challenge is to express it in productive, not destructive, ways. Anger can be expressed in nonaggressive ways and channeled into productive assertiveness. Expressing your anger nonaggressively will help you achieve your goals.

There is a dramatic difference between assertiveness and aggression. People that stand up for themselves are assertive, but people who hurt others in the process are aggressive. Express yourself assertively.

You may be frustrated with a policeman when he pulls you over for a traffic violation. But you do not grab him by his shirt collar and threaten him with aggression if he does not put the ticket pad away. You know that if you become aggressive there are far more dire consequences in store for you than receiving a ticket.

Frustration need not explode into aggression. One of the functions of the most recent evolutionary advance of the brain—our frontal lobes—is to inhibit blind aggression when not practical. In fact, people with frontal lobe damage have a great deal of difficulty restraining from aggressive behavior. Thanks to the frontal lobes, you are able to inhibit aggressive impulses.

Use your frontal lobes. If you feel that you have been wrongly treated at work, choose a practical, constructive, and productive way to channel your anger. Choose to file a grievance or arrange for a meeting with your supervisor and the person who offended you: confront them strategically.

To deal effectively with your anger, you will need to intercept the anger before you lash out so that you can:

1. Find out where the anger is coming from by asking yourself what about the situation disturbs you.
2. Ask yourself if there are any other emotions that anger is in fact covering up.

By examining the cause of your anger, you will be better able to understand yourself and insure that you do not distort your situation at work. Perhaps you are actually hurt, embarrassed, or humiliated by the situation. Anger could be a cover-up of other feelings, or a way of avoiding looking any deeper.

Joe discovered that the anger he felt toward his co-workers was misdirected. For weeks he had been trying to solve the computer-programming problem at work. His co-worker, Peter, managed to find the glitch in the system and presented it to the supervisor. The supervisor sang the praises of Peter and added the comment, "I wish we had more people like Peter."

Joe saw red. He wondered if his supervisor was criticizing him. He did not find the glitch; Peter did. Then Joe wondered if he said something to Peter that gave him the idea of how to fix the glitch. Joe thought, "Now Peter gets the credit."

A few days later Joe saw his supervisor and Peter enjoying a good laugh together in the break room. When Joe walked by neither of them acknowledged him. An hour later Joe saw Peter at the water cooler and both bumped into one another. Water spilled on Joe's shirt.

Peter said, "Oh, I'm sorry Joe. I didn't see you."

Joe snapped back, "Sure you didn't!"

Peter walked away shaking his head and saying, "What's got into you?"

Joe felt as though Peter had slapped him in the face.

That night he told his wife about the situation. She asked, "Why blame Peter?

"What do you mean? Don't you see that he and that poor excuse for a supervisor are putting me down?"

"Maybe your supervisor. But I'd think twice about Peter. How many years have you guys been friends?"

"Ten years, and he's thrown it all away!"

"Joe, I think you're the one who's throwing it away."

Joe took a hard look at himself. He realized that Peter didn't really do anything to warrant his anger. He was really angry with himself for not discovering the computer glitch.

Had Joe taken a step back and appraised his situation after Peter found the solution or the supervisor made the comment, he may not have overreacted to Peter when they bumped into one another. Had the collision occurred two weeks previously, both would have enjoyed a laugh together. Because Joe did not take a step back, he made the situation worse.

There are several mind traps that could fuel your anger and distort a frustrating situation. When you begin to get angry, it is harder to think clearly about all of the possible sources of your anger. There is greater risk of setting yourself up for a mental "knee jerk" mind trap. These mind traps are like sinkholes that are hard to think yourself out of, because in the heat of anger thoughts are narrowed. The following are typical mind traps that occur almost automatically if you don't resist their pull:

- **Exaggeration**: In the heat of anger your emotions are mobilized to lash out. If you lock into one frame, your anger stokes up and magnifies. In the heat of an argument you may think, "Well this blows the entire relationship."

- **Pseudotelepathy/mind reading**: When angry at someone, you may have the tendency to read into his ill intent and come to the conclusion that he meant to hurt you. In such a situation you may think, "He has been out to get me for years. I can see it in his face."

- **Crude labeling**: There is a need to categorize, to make sense of what you see and hear. When in a state of anger you gravitate to crude categories of blacks and whites. You may think, "This guy is a jerk."

- **Shoulds and Shouldn'ts**: Anger can mobilize your energy to react because your are faced with the dilemma of what to do and how to act. Because anger fuels your self-righteousness, those options are narrowed into shoulds and shouldn'ts. You may think, "They should fire my co-worker for what he has done."

- **Blaming**: Perhaps you feel that your supervisor gave you an assignment as a punishment. You may think, "If it wasn't for him giving me this stupid task I would not be in this mess." All the energy you waste blaming him may be reinvested into coming up with a way to either finish the job, ask for help, or delegate some of the tasks to co-workers.

- **Globalizing**: You may feel so overwhelmed with anger about how you have been treated at work that you think that the entire job is terrible. Perhaps you are feeling like the "fall guy" in your department. You may say to yourself, "If I stay here any longer, *they* will punish me further."

- **Self-righteousness**: If you feel that your supervisor is incompetent, do not let him know of your opinion. If you do express your opinion self-righteously, it is probable that you will draw fire. To make matters worse, when he defends himself, he will probably respond angrily, increasing the chances that you will respond to anger with your own. You may think to yourself, "How dare he dump on me! He is the incompetent one." On the other hand, if you *tactfully* express your critique by making helpful suggestions, you may be considered a valued employee not an irritant.

- **Whining**: If you find yourself complaining with side comments such as, "Why do I always get the crap around here," you will build a reputation as a whiner. By whining you will misplace your anger and probably suffer negative scrutiny. Instead, ask directly for a meeting for clarification of job assignments.

Make sure that you do not use anger as a weapon. Try not to use anger to take revenge on someone. Do not dump your anger on someone because you think he or she needs to be punished for something he or she has done. And do not use anger to keep your boss from giving you more work. Using anger as a weapon will result in more complicated problems for you in the future.

At all costs, avoid making blunders that show provocation. Self-defeating blunders can result in more job stress. For example, absolutely avoid the following:

- **Direct put-downs**: "You are worthless."
- **Profanity**: "I don't give a sh**."
- **Teasing**: "When are you going to catch up with the rest of us?"
- **Ultimatums**: "This is your last chance!"

One of the main problems with expressing your anger inappropriately is that it can snowball. If you confront your boss or co-worker angrily, you may find that the situation quickly escalates into an explosive event. You say something that he finds insulting; then he may respond by "upping your ante."

Though you cannot control how anyone will respond to your expression of anger, you can avoid setting off a chain of events. Even if you respond in what you regard as the subtlest way possible but punctuate your feelings with a sigh, the situation can snowball. Try to avoid the following:

- Shaking your head.
- Rolling your eyes.
- Sighing.
- Groaning.

- Waving your hand away.
- Sarcastic tones.
- Scowling.
- Finger pointing or making a fist.

Try instead to use:

- Humor.
- Letting go.
- Negotiation.
- Assertiveness.

These points can be illustrated by the example of how two police officers handled the same situation differently. Officers Buster and Smootha were not pleased with the recent transfer of Sergeant Dunkin into their squad. Dunkin was prone to assigning cases indiscriminately. Buster felt that he finally had enough. When Dunkin told him to go out and take a report of a neighborhood dispute over a fence, he could not restrain himself. Buster rolled his eyes and groaned saying, "Why the #!*@ me?"

Sergeant Dunkin knew he was in a position now in which he had to demonstrate authority. He said, "Well, Buster, are you saying that you are refusing the assignment?"

Buster snapped back sarcastically while looking at his peers, "I'm just tired of all the #!*@ assignments."

Dunkin responded by saying, "You will hear from me in writing." Then he walked over to Officer Smootha and made the same request.

Everyone in the room braced themselves for another confrontation. But they were all amazed by what happened. Instead of following Buster's approach, Officer Smootha said, "Well if I'm down there without backup, it's going to be tough. Tell you what Sergeant, if I go down there and break up that firefight in that neighborhood, can I have a direct line to the SWAT team?" Everyone broke out into laughter. As Sergeant Dunkin said, "Thanks Smootha," in laughter Smootha countered by saying, "Sure Sergeant but, can I get a safer assignment next time?"

Dunkin broke a sly smile and said, "I get it. Sure, I won't give you this kind of assignment next time." Then he looked at Buster to punctuate the point.

While Buster created more job stress for himself, Smootha managed to turn a bad situation to his advantage. Not only did he get an agreement that he would receive a more appealing assignment next time, but he also used his humor to set up an easygoing relationship with his new supervisor.

One common technique taught in anger management classes is referred to as "time out." When you feel the rage building, it is not time to talk. With rage surging, you are more vulnerable to ignite the situation into an angry confrontation. Avoiding angry confrontations may require that you step away from the situation to "collect yourself." Only after you step away and compose yourself can you reengage the person in communication. Try saying, "We need to talk about this, but I can see now is not the right time," or "I want to talk to you later about this." Then leave. Do not return until the surge of rage has died down.

If you are steaming with anger at your supervisor because he didn't give you the promotion you had sought, you can deal with the disappointment and anger destructively or constructively. Ironically, the destructive route is difficult to resist. For example, because you are angry, you can vent your anger with comments to everyone around you:

- "What is the use of trying? No good turn goes unpunished."
- "I'm through trying around here!"

If you take this approach, you will only garner negative scrutiny. Also, you could sabotage any promotion you might receive in the future.

Instead of wallowing in your anger and grief over not getting the promotion, do not give up. Go to your supervisor and try to make it clear that you are hoping to learn from the experience and want to know what steps you can take so that such a promotion is possible in the future. By taking this approach, you will demonstrate that the promotion is still a very important goal. Ask him to spell out the reasons for his decision and map out a course for you to follow to attain the goal in the future. With the course outlined, you will be in a better position to earn the promotion in the future or argue that you had done everything that he had required.

Focus on preparing yourself for the next opportunity. Find out which factors led to being passed over for a promotion and do your best to make those changes. If learning a specific skill, such as another language or the computer, will improve your chances, devote your energies to learning that skill. Do not give up. Keep in mind the following points:

- There will always be other opportunities.
- You can always improve your skills.
- Learning new skills can be vitalizing.
- Management is always impressed with people who refuse to give up while keeping a positive attitude.

When communicating with people who easily take offense, the best policy is to use "I" messages. An "I" message makes a statement without laying blame. In contrast, a "you" message can be interpreted as an offensive comment. For example, when talking to your boss you make either of two comments:

- **"I" message:** "I've been feeling really stressed lately with the deadline coming."
- **"You" message:** "Things could be better if you had not made this deadline."

The "you" message will probably result in your boss feeling insulted. He will be less inclined to look at your needs and more inclined to defend his own ego. With the "I" message, you cannot only appeal to his sympathy but also open the door to his possible help.

You can improve the interactions with co-workers and supervisors at work by using "active listening" techniques. When using active listening you should suspend your judgment and listen with empathy. Active listening involves repeating portions of what they have said such as, "Oh, so you have been feeling really stressed lately. Looks like we have something in common."

This approach lets the other person know that you are in fact listening. With active listening, you can acknowledge the most important points that the other person has said. Watch your body language to insure that you are conveying openness.

The combination of using both "I" messages and active listening will help you navigate through particularly challenging social situations. That is what Bart found. After one of the pipefitters was killed last month during an explosion at the refinery, Bart and his co-workers struggled to stay focused on the job. Everyone seemed to react differently to the death. To compound the problem, management at the refinery did nothing to acknowledge the grief that everyone felt. Bart, Frank, and Joe witnessed the horrible event but had not spoken about it. After feeling very frustrated with everyone's silence, Bart walked up to Frank during a break and said, "Looks like you are having a hard time getting back on track since it happened."

Frank recoiled and said, "What do you mean? I'm doing okay. What about you? You don't seem to be doing so good. You missed welding a whole seam yesterday."

Now Bart felt attacked, "Hey, you weren't there to back me up."

"Come on Bart! Get off my back," growled Joe.

Both men clammed up and walked back to their respective projects. Bart felt worse than he did before he talked to Frank. He wondered why his attempt to talk blew up in his face.

On his way home that night he stopped at a bookstore. He bought a book on communication. After dinner he read about "I" and "you" messages and active listening. He practiced these techniques with his wife.

The next day he approached Frank saying, "Look, Frank, yesterday when I asked you about how you were doing, I meant that I had been having a hard time dealing with the death I thought you may be feeling like I do."

Frank said, "Well, yeah I feel terrible. I don't want you to take this wrong but, it's a relief to hear that I'm not the only one. I haven't been getting much sleep either."

"Oh, sorry to hear that you haven't been sleeping."

The tension melted between the two men. Soon both were providing support to their co-workers.

Just as Bart managed to clear up the misunderstanding he carried and dissolve the tension between his friends and him, you also can avoid misunderstandings before they turn into major sources of conflict. Use "I" messages whenever possible and work on developing clarity between you and your co-workers.

Road Rage

In recent years, many people have added to their commute to work by moving farther out into the suburbs. The increasing cost of real estate in the population centers has meant that many people commute as much as two hours to work. In the San Francisco Bay Area, for example, families have moved as much as 70 miles away from the city because of the exorbitant cost of homes.

Highway construction has not kept up with the increase in the number of cars on the road. Drivers have not coped well with the congestion. It is not uncommon to see drivers cut one another off, then overreact as if they were almost killed. Obscene gestures fly and sometimes guns are even pulled. I once had an appointment with a man who was pulled over after he overreacted to another driver. He was so angry that he was finally arrested after assaulting the police officer.

This increase in commute time and the tension among drivers has meant that workers have endured considerable stress before they even arrive at work. You can feel emotionally exhausted and drained of energy just as you pull into the company parking lot. As a result of this stress, commuters have less energy to cope with stress on the job.

This stress may spill over into tension between co-workers who have all endured difficult commutes but end up dumping their resentment onto one another. The entire cascade of tension too often results in overreactions and misunderstandings between colleagues.

So what is a commuting worker to do if he cannot shorten the commute? How can the commute serve as a relaxing time rather then a harassing time? There are actually several adjustments you can make to your commute:

1. *Take a mass transit vehicle.* Utilize the light rail, bus system, or ferry system if one exists. Many companies organize ride pools. If none of these options are available, many towns organize van pools. Any of these options can contribute to financial savings, a time to get to know people more closely that you may not have had the chance to know, and/or a time to just sit back, relax, sleep, or read.

2. If possible, *change your schedule* to miss peak commute times.

3. Use the time in the car to *listen to books on tape or lectures* on subjects that you may have complained that you had never the time for in the past. I, for example, have been listening to several unabridged novels that I regularly check out from the library.

4. *Use relaxation exercises* that do not require you to close your eyes. As you sit and drive and watch your breath, you can also watch the ebb and flow of the traffic as if you are not a participant but an observer.

5. *Bring your favorite music tapes or CDs* and flow through traffic while listening to music.

Try any or all of these techniques. Don't let your commute throw tension into your workday. Make sure that when you arrive at work you are fresh and ready to deal with the demands of the day.

CHAPTER 9

Job Burnout

YOU MAY NOT SUFFER FROM job stress because of harassment, conflict with co-workers, too much work, or from the other obvious contributors to job stress. But you may still feel frustrated with your job. You are therefore left with a troubling question: "Is it me or is it the job?" The answer may be that you are suffering from job burnout.

Job burnout can occur for a variety of reasons. But most of all it occurs with people who have lost interest and motivation for the job. If you are burned out at your work, productivity may decrease, you may find yourself less flexible, and may have been told that you give your co-workers a down feeling.

Some of the main symptoms of burnout include:

- A lack of control over your job.
- Detachment from others.
- An increasing tendency to think negatively.
- A loss of energy and purpose.

Job burnout can result from a lack of variety or challenge. Burnout results from feeling that the job is stale; it may be boring, uninspiring, and uninteresting. It can also result from being stretched beyond any interest of your own, being overextended, or feeling a lack of purpose. Job burnout can occur if you:

- Are co-dependent. In other words, if you have difficulty delegating tasks and accept the jobs of others.
- Have difficulty saying no to new requests or commitments that you know you cannot accomplish.

- Feel that your job is repetitive, monotonous, and feels like Chinese water torture.
- Have held the same job responsibilities for several years without any rotations.

You can avoid job burnout by making sure that you find a sense of fulfillment in your work. Although this is certainly easier said than done, there are a number of steps that you can take to buffer yourself against burnout by rekindling a sense of enjoyment in your work. It will help if you consider the following points:

- Review your commitments and decide which of those are beyond your ability, time, and desire to complete.
- Prioritize your goals both professionally and personally.
- Eliminate or resign from those commitments that do not meet your goals.
- Tactfully say no to new requests that are not consistent with your goals and ability.
- Try to make sure that you can rotate tasks and instill variety in your work, thus avoiding monotony and boredom.

Do not be afraid to think about retraining or changing jobs. You need to think of yourself as portable. In other words, you are not your job and may benefit by trying to envision yourself changing occupations. The term "occupation" refers to what you have been occupied doing, not your core identity.

A dramatic example of job shift was modeled by one of my supervisees. She started her career as a ventriloquist. After oversleeping into her debut time on *The Ed Sullivan Show*, she found a career shift critical. She returned to college and earned a masters degree in art history. She taught art history at a state university for a few years and decided she needed a change. She went to law school and became a lawyer. But after awhile she decided she was more interested in her clients' personal problems then she was the legal process. She therefore went back to school and earned a masters degree in social work and became a social worker. Then she decided that she was just scratching the surface and therefore decided to pursue a doctorate in psychology.

If you cannot rotate your responsibilities, cannot switch jobs, and have no other job options, how can you recover from job burnout? To begin with, you can see your job with new eyes. Because everything we do and see is a matter of perspective and no two people experience the same job situation the same way, it may be time to change your perspective. You can try to see your job in a new light. Are there parts of your job that you have yet to notice? In what ways have you not yet tried to perform the same duties?

One way of changing your focus from a negative frame of reference to a positive one is to lose yourself in the task at hand. For example, if you are a factory worker who engages in the same repetitive task, you can use the time to meditate. The type of meditation that I am referring to here is called "mindfulness meditation." Though I will describe meditation in detail in Chapter 18, the point here is that if you pay very close attention to every movement of your body, you can become so absorbed in your movements that you will find the old job becomes a new job. Zen philosophers have been known to say, "Zen is not like chopping wood, Zen *is* chopping wood." In other words, you can both transcend and lose yourself in a simple task.

Charles experienced job burnout until he changed his perspective. For several years he felt that his job was going nowhere. He dreaded going to work on Monday. It was not as if he found any part of his job demanding. He just felt worn down. He wondered why he felt so stressed by a job that appeared to have no stress. As an insurance adjuster for the same company for the past 10 years, he was learning nothing new. There were no new challenges, all of his co-workers were the same, and there were few regulation changes. After hours of self-reflection, the only reason for his ill feelings about work seemed to be that he was terribly bored.

He could no longer keep his symptoms of his stress from home. He became irritable with his children and occasionally verbally abusive toward his wife. She finally said, "I can't take it anymore. What has got into you?"

"I'm just sick of my job."

"Well do something about it! Don't take it out on me and the kids."

Charles knew he had to do something, but he had no idea what. He scheduled an appointment with the employment assistant counselor,

Ms. Trainer. She told him about the company's tuition reimbursement program. To his amazement, his company actually promoted retraining even if it had nothing to do with skills that could be used at work. Ms. Trainer said that management had decided long ago that the only way to keep good employees was to help them grow. He decided to take part in the program. Within a few weeks, he felt a sense of enthusiasm quietly stirring.

Your employer may not have such a program, but you can still follow Charles' example. Check out the local community college or adult school. Find out what classes you can take in the evenings or on weekends.

Don't wait for your employer to save you from your job burnout. Take action to enrich yourself outside of work and on the job itself.

CHAPTER 10

Medicine and Herbs

WE ARE A PILL-ORIENTED CULTURE. If you have a headache, your first impulse may be to go to the medicine chest and take an aspirin. You may not try to discover why you have a headache. Perhaps you are dehydrated and need to drink water; perhaps you have consumed too much coffee and sugar or gone without a meal. If you feel anxiety or depression about your job, you would be far better of exploring methods of dealing with the anxiety without having to resort to a pill.

Nevertheless, assuming that you have exhausted all natural remedies, some medications may be helpful for dealing with anxiety and depression. What follows therefore is meant to help you navigate the complex sea of information (and/or lack of it) about medications and herbs.

Benzodiazepines

If you go to your primary care physician and complain that you are "stressed out" and full of anxiety, he or she may give you a medication that calms you down. But it's critical to remember that in the era of managed care, primary care physicians are overworked and some will feel compelled to prescribe something quick without fully assessing your problems. The type of medication that will probably be prescribed will be one of the benzodiazepines (benzos).

The benzodiazapines include Valium, Librium, Ativan, and Xanax. These drugs act on the neurotransmitter GABA, which serves to inhibit specific neurons from firing. They are therefore referred to as "minor tranquilizers" or as antianxiety agents. They are the most prescribed and the most addicting drugs in the United States. They are also more difficult to withdraw from than heroin. People have been known to have seizures and die as a result of abruptly withdrawing from high levels of Valium.

Some benzodiazapines may be helpful. When taken on a short-term basis, if dietary and psychological methods have been exhausted and you are feeling overwhelmingly anxious in the late evening, a low dose of a short-term prescription of a drug like Ativan may be helpful. Ativan, unlike its cousin Valium, has a short half-life. In other words, the effects of Ativan wear off sooner than Valium. At first glance you may think, "I don't want it to wear off quickly." But because Ativan does have a shorter half-life than Valium, it does not fog the mind as much as Valium does in the morning.

In addition to the anti-anxiety effects, benzos have a number of negative side effects. They have a tendency to make people depressed. You will not want to treat your anxiety by replacing it with depression. Benzos also have a tendency to contribute to deficits in clarity of thought and to dampen short-term memory. Clarity of thought and memory will be crucial for the development of coping strategies. Last but not least, the sleep benefit is short-lived and the quality of sleep you receive by taking a benzo is poor, as you will see in Chapter 17.

For all of these reasons, I seriously caution people to hesitate before asking their primary care physician for a prescription of a benzo. You want your job stress to fade away, not be complicated by side effects of a medication.

Antidepressants

If you complain of being depressed, your primary care physician may ask if you want to take an antidepressant medication. But be advised that most require weeks before you will feel any antidepressant effect. Thus, no one on the street sells antidepressants the way they sell the benzodiazapines. Antidepressant medications are also nonaddictive, and there are no adverse withdrawal dangers except depression.

There are three broad classes of antidepressant medications: the older tricyclic antidepressants (TCAs) such as Elavil; the monoamine inhibitors (MAO inhibitors) such as Parnate; and the newer selective serotonin reuptake inhibitors (SSRIs) such as Prozac.

The TCAs work on either serotonin or norepinephrine or both; the MAOs and the SSRIs work on serotonin exclusively. Only Welbutrin (in a class by itself) affects the neurotransmitter dopamine. It has been found that some people respond better to one type of medication and not as well to others. If your doctor gives you one type of medication and your friend raves about another, do not second-guess your physician's decision until you give the medicine time to work.

If you tell your doctor that in addition to your depression you are having trouble sleeping, she will probably prescribe a TCA like Elavil because of its sedative effects. The sedative effect occurs right away, but the antidepressant effect will take approximately four weeks to reach its full benefit.

MAO inhibitors require strict dietary restrictions. These drugs interact with certain foods containing tyramine, a natural by-product of bacterial fermentation processes. Thus, some wines, beers, pickled herring, chocolate, and chopped liver have been found to contribute to severe reactions. People who have taken MAOs and eaten foods with tyramine have experienced a severe hypertensive crisis. Nevertheless, despite the dietary caution, MAOs have been found to be effective in treating certain phobias and atypical depression.

The SSRIs are the new kids on the block. Prozac is the most well known but it has also received a lot of bad press. Much of the hype about the negative effects of Prozac is highly exaggerated. Despite the "bad rap," Prozac and its cousins Paxil and Zoloft have been shown to have very positive effects for many people. These drugs have also been helpful for some people who suffer from obsessive-compulsive disorder.

The SSRIs have a variety of side effects including nausea, nervousness, and butterflies-in-the-stomach feelings. Many of these side effects pass in time. But Prozac has been found to cause persistent insomnia in many people. It has also been found to cause impotence in men and to interfere with women reaching an orgasm.

The TCAs have what is referred to as "anticholinergic" side effects. These side effects include dry mouth, constipation, difficulty urinating, and blurry vision. Most of the TCAs cause some sedation. Elavil and Sinequan have the most sedation and Norpramin and Vivactil the lowest.

It is particularly important to avoid alcohol when using TCAs. The two together are a lethal combination. Many years ago, two people in one of my day treatment programs died because they combined the two.

All of these medications have side effects, and because of them many people quit the medication after a few days. Many physicians fail to warn patients that the medications have side effects that fade in time. This is why most antidepressant medications are "triturated" up in dose. In other words, because it takes your body time to adjust to the medication, your doctor will increase slowly to the desired dose.

If you begin to take an antidepressant medication, it is highly recommended that you take it for at least six months. These medications are not intended to be taken on an as-needed basis; in other words, you should *not* take them only on days that you feel depressed. They are meant to be taken as prescribed at the same time each day without missing a day; otherwise, the medication will not work.

Patsy experienced so much job stress that she considered medication. She erroneously assumed that her doctor would tell her everything she needed to know. She complained of job stress, offering no detail, nor did she ask for information from him after he prescribed 10 milligrams of Valium. She immediately felt calmer but soon began to feel more depressed then she had before. She went back to her doctor and told him that she felt so depressed that she now didn't feel like leaving the house. He said, "Oh, you didn't tell me that you were depressed." He referred her to a psychiatrist who had an office in the same building. The psychiatrist prescribed her 100 milligrams of Elavil.

After six weeks she returned and complained that not only did she feel just as depressed as she had before, but now she felt groggy and hated having a dry mouth in the morning and blurry vision. He said, "Well, some people don't respond so well to some medications and very well to others. I think that we ought to try Prozac. For the first week take 10 milligrams then go up to 20 milligrams on the second week. Because you had trouble sleeping, I want you to take the medication in the morning."

During the first week she was troubled with a queasy stomach, diarrhea, and insomnia. But she stuck it out and found that these side effects began to subside. After the fifth week, she was delighted because the depression was finally lifting.

Unlike Patsy, some people become so annoyed with the side effects of a medication that they quit and never return to that doctor. Other people continue taking the medication despite the side effects and fail to tell their doctor that it didn't work. For example, had Patsy not complained to her doctor that the Valium made her depressed, she may have dutifully continued taking it. Her job stress would have gotten worse because of her increase in depression.

If you take medication, be informed. Don't blindly take a medication without knowing its side effects or the common doses.

Table 10.1 shows some of the most common medications, their side-effects, and dosage ranges.

Brand	Generic	Dose Range	Sedation	ACH Side Effects*
Prozac	Fluoxetine	20-80	Low	None
Paxil	Paroxetine	20-50	Low	None
Zoloft	Sertraline	50-200	Low	None
Tofranil	Imipramine	150-300	Mid	Mid
Elavil	Amitriptyline	150-300	High	High
Norpramin	Desipramine	150-300	Low	Low
Pamelor	Nortiriptyline	75-125	Mid	Mid
Sinequan	Doxepin	150-300	High	Mid
Effexor	Venlafaxine	75-375	Low	None
Nardil	Phenelzine	30-90	Low	None
Parnate	Tranylcypromine	20-60	None	None

Anticholinergic side effects (dry mouth, blurry vision)

Table 10.1. Common Medications and Their Side Effects

Herbs

Recent surveys have found that more than half of Americans have used "alternative" healing techniques, including herbs. Although many of these herbs are quite helpful, they are not well researched, nor does the federal Food and Drug Administration (FDA) regulate them to insure their safety. The bottom line is that you do not know what you are getting when you buy herbs. Many herbs are marketed with grandiose claims, such as "boost your brain power" or "give yourself a lift."

There is far more written about herbs and their effects in Europe, particularly Germany, than found in the United States. A good source of information is the book *Rational Phytotherapy,* the result of research done in Germany. What follows is *not* meant to serve as prescribing guidelines for particular herbs but merely as a brief introduction. If you take herbs, it is strongly advised that you consult someone who knows your health history and understands herbology.

St. John's Wort

St. John's Wort is an herb that has been used for more than 2000 years. The genus "Hypericum" occurs throughout the world. It has been used in the treatment of mood disorders since the early 19th century. During the late 20th century, it has been used by large numbers of people in Germany. The mechanism of St. John's Wort is not well understood, but it is widely assumed to inhibit the reuptake of serotonin like the SSRIs, meaning that it makes serotonin more available.

Providing you have a good quality St. John's Wort extract, most guidelines recommend approximately 300 milligrams three times per day. Excessive doses of St. John's Wort have been noted to cause phototoxic skin reactions. If you take St. John's Wort, do not take any other medication that acts on serotonin because you can develop "serotonin syndrome."

St. John's Wort has fewer adverse side effects than many of the synthetic antidepressant medications. But like most antidepressant medications, you cannot expect a marked improvement in mood for several weeks. It is not suitable for daily use as a sedative or mood elevator.

Kava Kava

Kava is an herb originating in the South Pacific. Natives of Polynesia, Melanesia, and Micronesia harvested the large rhizome of the Kava shrub, masticated it, then mixed it with coconut milk and water to make a beverage. After consumption it produced a relaxing and calming effect, reportedly without clouding consciousness. Today Kava is cultivated all over the Pacific.

Kava apparently acts on the excitability of the limbic system, that area in the brain associated with mood. It produces an effect similar to the benzodiazapines. Generally, it is regarded as an herb that acts as an antianxiety agent and as a "tension reducer."

Many of the studies on Kava used doses of kava extract of 60-120 milligrams of kavapyrones daily. Toxic effects of Kava have been reported to include skin rash, yellowing of the skin, gastrointestinal complaints, redness of the eyes, respiratory problems, loss of appetite, and ataxia. Prolonged use of Kava has been associated with visual impairment, papillary dilation, and disturbances of oculomotor equilibrium.

Valerian

Valerian is one of the many sleep-inducing herbs sold in health food stores. There are approximately 250 species of Valerian found worldwide, but the European variety is the most researched. The Indian and Mexican varieties are associated with a higher therapeutic risk because of the high content of valepotriates. The European variety is identified by a strong odor. Take 2-3 grams of dried extract per day or 600 milligrams of the ethanol extract taken 2 hours before bedtime, as recommended by *Rational Phytotherapy: A Physician's Guide to Herbal Medicine*.

Valerian is thought to act by decreasing the degradation of GABA. In other words, it acts to facilitate GABA, which promotes a reduction of anxiety. But unlike Valium (diazepam), Valerian has been found to not impair deep sleep (theta wave sleep) or increase the shallow level of sleep (beta wave sleep).

Valerian is not recommended as an aid to produce immediate sleep effects. Many people report that it takes 2-4 weeks to produce positive effects. Thus, Valerian is not recommended as a treatment of acute insomnia.

Side effects and risks include headache, morning grogginess, and some geotoxic risk to the gastrointestinal tract and liver. Valerian products originating from Mexican or Indian sources should not be used due to mutagenic risk.

Mary was like many people who sought help from herbs instead of pharmaceuticals. Despite the fact that she suffered from depression during the past two years, she didn't want to seek professional help. She knew that her job was getting her down but she wasn't ready to make any changes. She read about Prozac in a news magazine and was hesitant to ask her doctor for a prescription.

Since adolescence, she frequented health food stores and tried to make sure that she maintained a good diet. She knew that many of her friends had used a variety of different herbs as a means of improving cognition, calming themselves, and as mood elevators. Her friend Barbara told her that St. John's Wort helped with depression.

Mary went to the health food store and asked the store owner to recommend a good quality bottle of St. John's Wort. After he recommended a reputable brand, he told her to take 300 milligrams three times a day.

Mary was disappointed that after two weeks she didn't feel any better. She went back to the store owner and complained that she must have a bad batch. The owner said, "Oh, I forgot to tell you that it takes about four weeks to have an effect."

Mary found that after two more weeks she was beginning to feel less depressed. She also found that things that had bothered her in the past seemed less offensive. She began to feel that she was ready to make the changes at work that had so long loomed over her like a dark cloud.

Whether you use herbs or medication to help you deal with job stress, do so as an informed consumer. If you don't pay close attention to the side effects and appropriate cautions associated with these compounds, your job stress may unknowingly increase. Finally, use the maxim: Less is more. In other words, if you really don't need to change your body chemistry, don't.

CHAPTER 11

Move and Feel Better

SEVERAL STUDIES HAVE SHOWN THAT people who exercise on a regular basis are better able to deal with stress. On the other hand, those who do not exercise on a regular basis and work in a sedentary job are at risk to suffer more stress and depression.

It has repetitively been demonstrated that exercise produces a "tranquilizing effect." Because of the biochemical changes occurring as a result of physical exertion, anxiety is muted. Exercise is a far better treatment than taking an antianxiety medication and has none of the negative side effects.

Exercise has numerous positive side effects. For example, exercise enhances oxygenation of your blood. When your blood is transported to your brain, you feel alert and calm. Exercise also lowers the acidity in your body, which increases your energy level.

There are many forms of exercise. Some involve a time commitment while others can be performed impulsively. You can stretch, walk, or perform an aerobic exercise such as running or bicycle riding. All of these promote relaxation and a greater sense of well-being.

Stretching

A considerable amount of energy is wasted in maintaining muscle tension. A person who suffers from job stress will feel "all wound up" with muscle tension and as a result will often feel fatigued. Chronic stress builds up in muscles, making tendons thicken and shorten due to overdevelopment of connective tissue. Stress contributes to the overactivity of the sympathetic nervous system, resulting in tension buildup in an already taxed system. The way to get rid of that buildup of tension is to stretch.

Many people work in environments that offer them little opportunity to move. Sedentary workplaces promote the tendency for stress to build up in our bodies. Because of the lack of movement, muscles tighten up and atrophy. This "body-stored" tension feeds on our stress level and contributes to more stress. In other words, the tension channeled into our bodies spills back over into more psychological tension because our bodies "feel tense."

People who experience stress have a tendency to tighten their muscles. For this reason methods of relaxing muscles need to be developed. An excellent way to drive out tension and relax your muscles is stretching.

Your muscles are endowed with a rich blood supply. Just as exercise promotes better blood flow to your muscles and results in the energized feeling of relaxation, so too can stretching. By stretching your muscles you are forcing or pumping the used and deoxygenated blood back for refueling in the lungs. This blood flow is complemented by the replenishment of reoxygenated blood out to your muscles. Stretching promotes refreshed and invigorated muscles and the release of tension.

The following stretching techniques can provide instantaneous treatment for stress, and they can be performed anywhere.

The Chest Expander

Stand with your arms at your sides. Keeping your hands separated, raise your arms and breathe deeply. Without dropping your arms inhale and exhale as many slow deep breaths as you can. Repeat the exercise at least three times.

The Shoulder Shrug

Raise your shoulders up to your ears. Now roll your shoulders back. Imagine your shoulder blades touching. Now drop your shoulders. Repeat the movements several times, timing those movements to deep breathing. This exercise releases tension stored in your shoulders and upper back.

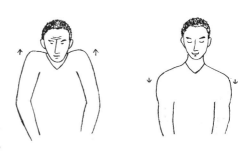

The Neck Roll

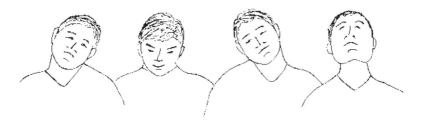

Drop your chin to your chest and roll your head clockwise all the way around until your head is in the same position as it was when you began. Now roll your head in the counterclockwise direction. The neck roll will help you release tension built up in your neck, head, and shoulders.

Prayer/Hand Push

Place your hands together in a prayer position close to your chest. Push both hands together with elbows pointing outwards. Breathe deeply.

Fist Clenching

Clench your hands into fists. Then let go and extend your fingers as far and as wide as you can.

Moving

Most people who do not exercise are unwilling to admit that it is really their laziness that impedes them. Often they have developed an array of rationalizations. If you do not exercise on a regular basis you may have chosen one of the following reasons:

Reason	Contradiction
• I don't have the time.	• But you may have enough time to watch television.
• I don't belong to any gyms.	• But most forms of exercise can be done outside of a health club.
• I'm not athletic.	• Walking or running requires no athletic ability.
• I can't walk in my neighborhood.	• Most people have cars. You can easily drive to a park.

Many people who are depressed say, "I'm just too tired to exercise." What they do not realize is that exercising actually will increase their energy level over time. For example, it has been demonstrated that just 10 minutes of exercise will boost a hormone called epinephrine, which will increase your energy level and give you positive feelings.

Walking is the easiest, cheapest, and the most natural form of exercise available to you. You can walk around your neighborhood, at a regional park, or on a treadmill at your local health club. Several studies have shown that people who walk become less depressed. For example, if we take a group of depressed people and divide them up into a group that walks and a non-walking group, insuring that neither group receives any type of treatment for their depression, we find that the group that walks becomes less depressed. Walking is antidepressant.

Exercising forces your amnergic system to increase output because more norepinephrine is needed to rev up the heart rate. This charge up of norepinephrine occurs also in the brain. As noted earlier, some antidepressant medications work to increase the transmission of nore-pinephrine.

For the past 30 years, people have talked about the so-called "runners high." This feeling of well-being is the result of the release of the body's endorphins, which are natural brain opioids. Not only do we experience a euphoric mellow feeling after we exercise, but stress hormones are reduced.

It's not uncommon for people who had exercised on a regular basis to stop when they experience job stress. Tim was one of these people. He had been an avid runner before he began to feel burdened by job stress. He said to himself, "I just don't have the energy for it anymore." Then he abruptly stopped running.

Gradually, he became more depressed. At work he found that he was tense all of the time. He no longer felt that nice glowing feeling he had in the evening after running. He found himself worrying about little things that occurred during the day at work.

As he tried to go to sleep each night, his wife noticed that he tossed and turned. In the morning he felt exhausted.

His wife said, "You were so much more relaxed when you were running. Why don't you just get out there again."

"I'm just too stressed out and tired for that. I'll get back to it when I feel better."

"Just try it," she implored.

After work that evening he put on his running shoes and managed to run his usual distance. As he sat down for dinner he was delighted to feel that familiar glow again. After a week of running each evening he found that his sleep had improved and he seemed to regain his old energy level. He no longer felt exhausted when he woke up in the morning. At work he was better able to cope with his job stress.

Tim's sleep improved because his exercise forced his impaired sleep back into a normal cycle, in part because the aminergic neurotransmitters are better able to control rapid eye movement (REM) sleep. (Sleep will be discussed in great detail in Chapter 17, including how to exercise to maximize sleep).

If you work in a sedentary workplace and afford yourself no exercise, you need to develop ways to drain off the physical tension. Stress-reducing exercise does not mean going to an expensive health club, suiting up in expensive workout gear, or running five miles a day. Any kind of exercise is great and can take any form. Even strenuous yard work can result in the aerobic boost. The following activities can help:

- Raking the leaves.
- Shoveling snow.
- Walking the dog.
- Digging a hole.
- Climbing stairs instead of using elevators.
- Riding your bicycle or walking to work.
- Vacuuming the house.
- Scrubbing the floor.

One of the films shown on rainy days to high school physical education classes features a man who is so depressed that he wants to kill himself. This man decides that the best way to kill himself would be to run as long as he could in order to induce a heart attack. One day he tried to run beyond being exhausted but did not die or have a heart attack. The next day he tried again and ran farther, but still he did not die. Each day he tried to run farther but he did could not die! Soon he found that he began to feel differently. He no longer felt suicidal. In fact, his depression began to lift! The man decided to keep on running, not in an attempt to kill himself, but to keep from killing himself.

CHAPTER 12

Surviving Tech Stress

HIGH-TECH GADGETRY HAS MADE many workplaces more stressful than ever. E-mails, faxes, and cell phone calls all demand our attention—right now! What do you answer first? Confusion, frustration, and panic rush in where certainty, calm, and clarity ought to be.

According to a Yankee Group Survey, more than 50 percent of the workforce uses high technology. And if you feel frazzled by its breakneck pace, you have plenty of company. A study done by the Institute for the Future found that employees for Fortune 1,000 companies send and receive 178 messages each day by communication technologies. In addition, 84 percent of these employees say that they are interrupted on average three times per hour.

Our brains just aren't designed to deal with this communication overload. In their book *Techno-stress,* Larry Rose and Michelle Weil say that being bombarded with information produces increased irritability, low frustration tolerance, difficulty concentrating, a feeling of disconnection with oneself and others, and free-floating anxiety. David Lewis refers to this spectrum of symptoms as "Information Fatigue Syndrome."

If these symptoms sound all too familiar, you are suffering from tech stress. This chapter can help you recognize and cope with it, showing you how to make technology your slave instead of your master.

Age and Tech Stress

If you're feeling stressed trying to keep up with the workload on your Visual Display Terminal (VDT) or computer, you may wonder why your younger colleagues seem to be breezing along. Many studies have shown that younger workers have an easier time adjusting to the advent of the new technologies than do older workers.

Some people have argued that young people have familiarity with computers, adding to their greater comfort and skill level. Certainly familiarity increases anyone's competence level. But there is a another reason why you as an older worker have a more difficult time with computers than your younger counterparts. Older adults have been found, in study after study, to undergo declines in their cognitive capacities.

Psychologists have been amassing test results of people from different age groups for more than 100 years. The following list includes some of the main age-related declines relevant to VDT and computer use:

1. Short-term memory.
2. Processing speed.
3. Attention/concentration.
4. Visual perception and processing.
5. Problem solving.

Of critical interest to the use of the new technologies is the fact that you will have diminishing capacities in processing complex and confusing stimuli and allocating your attention to task-relevant information. This problem is especially pronounced if the information is new and presented in an unfamiliar or complex domain such as on a computer. To make matters worse, you will find that there is a decreased processing speed. Because you experience a general slowing in processing speed, other thinking abilities are dampened because you find it harder to get information integrated. In other words, as new information has to be processed such as in a computer domain, you are slower than younger adults on computer tasks.

What psychologists have called "working memory," commonly referred to as short-term memory, declines with age. Working memory is a very important part of many computer tasks. When you work on the computer you must hold information in your mind, while simultaneously using a mental model of an unfamiliar system, then use a sequence of commands such as tracking complex databases or file records. You have to remember what information is contained in which file, then perform calculations or manipulations of the information to arrive at a reasonable solution to a problem.

To compensate for the problems of declining attention and working memory when using the computer, make liberal use of the text editor and pull-down menus. Ask a tech support person to format your tabletop with a box with a list of on-screen cues. This "cheat sheet" will save you a lot of time and frustration. Once you have all of the cues memorized, you can "minus-out" or close the box.

Because the work on VDT and computers require constant visual attention for extended periods of time, you are probably well aware that your eyesight is not what it used to be. Many people can't read without eyeglasses by their mid-forties. You also require more time to read from VDTs. The degree and type of lighting can have an influence on your fatigue and the propensity to get headaches. But eyesight is not the only problem related to visual decline.

As you age, you will also have difficulty with tasks that require divided attention. For example, if you are managing several windows of information and have to shift your attention back and forth between windows, your ability to work with accuracy and speed will probably lag behind the performance of younger adults.

This is because you will experience age-related declines in visual search abilities and capacity to attend to relevant information without being distracted. Therefore, you may find the images confusing and have trouble deciding what to pay attention to and what task to perform next. You may feel that at times you are "lost in hyperspace."

To compensate for the visual limitations, it is advisable to gain tech support to construct your "task environment" in such a way that would be free from visual disruptions and distractions. Make sure that what appears on your screen is arranged in such a way that you are cued to the highest priorities first.

When taking on challenges such as time-pressured data entry, you make more mistakes than younger workers when speeding up to work faster than your comfort level. To compensate for these difficulties, you might try to insure that you reduce the pacing requirement and take breaks. Because you probably do much better if you are familiar with the tasks, make sure that you take advantage of any training that may be available. Even though the last thing you want to do is more work, practice the task when there is no time pressure so that you can build up your comfort level before going back to work.

Because stress impacts the body, older adults take longer to recover from the effects of stress then do younger adults. Measures of arousal such as the levels of epinephrine and norepinephrine, which go up with stress and may be linked to heart disease, take longer to go down for older adults. Therefore, take frequent breaks to insure that you are pacing yourself maximally.

Advancing age often includes a tendency to be more cautious and careful; therefore, the sense of being in control is critically important. Whereas machine-paced tasks are externally controlled, a self-paced information flow is internally controlled. Thus, the difference between a machine-paced and a self-paced rate of information to process means the difference between uncontrollable stress and manageable stress. Try when possible to organize your tasks to be self-paced.

Your workstation can be organized so poorly that you are distracted by physical discomfort. In addition to poor lighting, your desk and keyboard may prevent you from reaching and sitting comfortably for several hours a day. Also, if your chair is not adjustable or doesn't provide you with enough support, you may be experiencing unnecessary disc pressure. All of these physical discomforts detract from your ability to focus on the complexity of your VDT or computer screen.

One clear finding from research with older adults is that prior computer experience helps to bolster your self-confidence and efficiency. Prior experience cultivates a deeper knowledge of the domain of computers, and it's in the realm of "deep knowledge" that older adults excel. With your expanded knowledge of the computer domain, not only will your comfort level go up, but you will take pride in the work that you perform.

To maximize your computer and VDT skills, do the following:

- Practice, practice, practice.
- Take classes in computer skills when possible.
- Format your tabletop with a cheat sheet.
- Take breaks and rest your eyes.
- Try to develop a self-paced format.

- Make sure that your rate and display of information doesn't needlessly involve too many windows open at the same time.
- Arrange your workstation to maximize ergonomic comfort and efficiency.

Although many of the age-related declines in mental abilities relevant to computer use can't be totally ameliorated, incorporate the preceding recommendations to minimize your limitations and maximize your efficiency and enjoyment in your work.

Don't Get Cyberspaced

There is an increasingly surreal interface between you and your computer the more hours you spend staring into the screen. Not only are your eyes strained looking into the artificial light but the tangible reality of physical sensation, the feel of paper, the sound of a typewriter, and the conversation with people are lost as you drift off into cyberspace. MIT computer sociologist Sherry Turkle has pointed out that computers don't provide the "transparency" necessary for you to understand how they work. In other words, you can't "see" what makes your computer work because there are no exposed gears or tangible functioning parts. You may rely on psychological terms to understand what the computer does and does not do.

For example, when stressed the boundary between you and your computer may become defused. You may project human intention on it by saying, "What's this thing up to! It won't let me get to my e-mail!" It's best to take a break when you reach this level of frustration. If you continue to try to work on your computer when highly frustrated, chances are you will make even more mistakes. Try the following:

- Walk away for a few minutes to clear your mind.
- Ask a co-worker to talk you through simple commands.
- Pull out a manual and follow the steps one by one.
- Call your tech support and have her explain how you can move from one command to another.

Working with computers and VDTs can also incite fear. All over the United States and in Europe workers have expressed fears of developing health problems because of being exposed to electromagnetic fields associated with VDTs and computers. People have complained of neurological, mucous membrane, and dermatological symptoms that they feel have been caused by their VDT or computer. These reports are so prevalent in Sweden that some people have quit work and moved out into the "woods" to get away from any exposure to electromagnetic fields.

Workers in Norway were the first to report that their VDT caused skin problems including rosacealike dermatitis, seborrhoeic eczema, and erythema. Yet research on these people failed to find any correlation between their VDT and their dermatological problems. In fact, research related to all of the VDT-caused physical complaints has yet to verify that it as the cause. Some of this research was done by using the "double blind" approach, meaning participants didn't know who was the control group or the exposed group until the measurements were completed.

Some have argued that the problems are psychosomatic, meaning that the fear related to the VDTs and computers stir the symptoms. This has been called a "vicious circle" wherein a person's fear of being exposed increases their symptoms, which as a result increases their fear. The bottom line for tech workers is that the jury is still out, and needless worrying about an affliction that has yet to be verified will cause undo tech stress.

There are, however, well-verified health problems as a result of working at computers or VDTs, such as musculoskeletal aches including sore necks and backs. Most studies have found that a preponderance of women who report upper limb work-related musculoskeletal disorders (WMSD). This disparity in the incidence of WMSD is primarily due to the fact that more women than men use the keyboard.

Also, your eyes may be strained because you are constantly staring into the artificial light of the monitor. You may find that it's especially difficult to look at your computer screen because of the glare and poor lighting. Because of the eyestrain, you may find yourself getting headaches throughout the day. Try to attach a non-glare shield onto your screen. Make sure that you have proper lighting, that is over the computer and not behind you. Make sure that your reading glasses are appropriate.

Jobs that require heavy computer use are generally sedentary, and because of less physical movement you may experience a dramatic increase in tension building up in your body. Make sure that you get up to walk around and get your blood circulating more efficiently.

You may think that it is only during the initial learning phase of computer work that you suffer stress. Yet recent research on the prolonged effects of repetitive and monotonous work such as data entry raises the levels of stress-related neurotransmitters such as epinephrine and norepinephrine, and they stay high long after the end of your regular workday. Increases in cortisol also remain high if you suffer already from higher heart rates and blood pressure.

To compound the stress related to using the new technologies, some workers have felt additional stress as a result of excessive workloads, rotating shifts, role confusion, and monotonous or repetitive tasks. One way to combat the monotony of repetitive work is to enlarge the scope of the job by combining simple tasks with complex tasks. The increase in variety reduces the psychological boredom. A slight modification of "job enlargement" approach is to alternate repetitive tasks with complex tasks. By using this method you could "rest" during repetitive phases before shifting back to phases with complex tasks and the need for higher order thinking.

Because stress affects not only you but also the work you do and the company you work for, your stress reduction program should involve organizational change. Thus, we now turn to how you can participate in humanizing the high-tech workplace.

Humanizing Tech Work

The advent of computers in the workplace has dramatically enhanced organizational functions such as document preparation, inventory management, and office scheduling. However, many of the benefits achieved by companies through computer automation are not always worker-friendly. For example, the following list includes gains achieved by the companies that greatly increase worker insecurity:

- A smaller workforce is needed.
- A less skilled and cheaper workforce is possible.
- An overall increase in quality and conformity of work is being performed.

Not surprisingly many workers have felt threatened by the computer-automated workplace. In study after study, workers report the following:

- Fear their job will be replaced by a computer.
- Feeling overwhelmed by the pressure of the workload.
- High time pressure demands.
- Frustration with the lack of decision-making opportunities.
- Less flexibility and the feeling of having to work under strict timelines.
- Lack of supervisory support.
- Frequent system breakdowns without prompt tech support.
- The decrease in contact with co-workers.
- The increase in musculoskeletal pain including repetitive stress injuries such as carpal tunnel syndrome.

If you are on the lowest level of the job stratum in your organization, chances are that you are more adversely affected by the advent of VDTs in your company than those at higher levels. Workers at your level have reported the most amount of stress related to social isolation and less cooperation. Also, job security is more tenuous at your level than those above you. Compared to those above you, your work is probably more monotonous and less gratifying. To make matters worse, because of the repetitiousness of the tasks you perform, there is a higher chance of physical discomfort. There has been a tenfold increase in repetitive stress injuries over the past decade.

By providing lower-level tech workers with a clear route of advancement through the organization, their work quality and morale can be bolstered. Training to achieve higher levels is critical. If you believe that you won't be doing the same repetitive tasks until retirement, everyone wins.

Many studies have found that the combination of task difficulty and poor supervision adds significant stress on workers using VDTs. Without good explanation and instruction, your feelings of fatigue and discomfort go up. Therefore, the stronger you advocate for instruction and confront your feelings of incompetence the better. If you don't make clear that you need support, your worst fear of being "found out" as incompetent would happen anyway.

Recent research has shown that the degree of psychological distress in workers is related to the design and organization of the computerized office work systems. Job design, management practices, organizational policies, and career opportunities dramatically influence how much stress you are going to endure.

Office employees that depend on constant access to their VDT or computer experience fatigue when they have to endure computer system breakdown, scheduling changes, and new applications. Insuring that you get prompt tech support will minimize the stress.

Because all of these problems are impacting you more than those above you, your participation on committees or your influence with your union should be directed toward recommending participation in goal setting, how the new technologies are brought in to the workplace, and job diversification.

If you get involved in a committee that is charged with balancing the demands of the work with the health of the workers, consider the following as important components to add to the plan:

• A sense of job control for the workers.
• Structured socialization opportunities during the workday.
• Reasonable production standards.
• Workers are involved in the decision making and goal setting.
• Flexible work schedule and rest breaks.
• On-the-stop tech support for breakdowns of the computer systems.
• Supervisory support that "buffer" workers from system problems.
• Enlargement of job task variety and the minimization of monotony.
• Opportunity for training and job advancement.

Avoiding Impersonal Communication

Today's workplace can be surreal and impersonal. Personal contact often is filtered through telecommunications gadgetry. You may "meet" with your co-workers for a phone conference. Possibly the only time you see some of them is during a videoconference.

Though these innovations may save companies millions of dollars, there is a human cost. The loss of face-to-face contact obliterates the subtle nuances of body language and makes it harder to develop personal relationships by shutting off the nonbusiness related talk that takes place during breaks.

For example, videoconferencing is eerily similar to watching a television show. Just as the actors play parts in a sitcom or soap opera, co-workers appear to one another as actors playing roles scripted by their job titles. In this surreal context, misunderstanding, projection, and personal alienation flourish.

If you are like most office workers, you start each day by turning on your computer, logging on, checking your e-mail and voice mail. Then, you probably check it over and over again throughout the day. Indeed, on many corporate networks a pop-up message interrupts you every time an e-mail, all too often labeled "urgent," lands in your mailbox. The first step in reducing your techn stress is to resist the feeling you must reply immediately.

First, if you let the warp speed of technology dictate your work pace, stress is inevitable. Human beings can't work at the speed of light. Second, if you reply to messages impulsively you will make mistakes, some of them whoppers.

So, put aside your e-mail until you can give it a block of time. Then, read and consider your reply to each one carefully. Make sure that your main points are up front and first. Do not be afraid to repeat yourself. Any misunderstanding can come back to haunt you. Above all, read over your e-mail before you press the send button.

Fred found himself in trouble because of his habit of responding to e-mail hastily. As an auto claims investigator for an insurance company, Fred receives many e-mails every day. One day he opened a newly arrived e-mail that read, "I didn't appreciate your obscene comment. You'll hear from my attorney!" It was signed Peggy Gernshaw. He had no idea what she meant, nor could he remember Peggy. He wondered if he had somehow made a flippant remark. He went to the sent folder and found that he had, in fact, received her e-mail at 10:55 a.m. two days ago in which she asked, "Can the paint be buffed out?" To his astonishment he had responded, "See you in the buff." He shook his head and tried to comprehend why he had written such a thing when his phone rang. It was his supervisor. He told Fred that a complaint had been filed against him.

Try to avoid Fred's mistake of replying impulsively to e-mail. Periodically make phone contact or meet with those people you frequently communicate with using e-mail. The personal contact will promote good relationships and immunize you from needless misunderstandings.

Surviving High-Tech Surveillance

Computers, cell phones, video monitors, and other high-tech equipment makes it relatively easy for employers to keep workers under surveillance. You don't have to look far to see that others are being watched. If you call for help of some kind you may hear a taped message that says, "This call may be monitored to ensure customer satisfaction."

If you are being watched closely by an electronic performance monitoring system (EPM), chances are you are feeling more stress then you ever had before. The EPM provides supervisors with intricate detail of your computer work, leaving you no flexibility or the feeling that you have no control over your job.

If you access the Internet through your company's network, there's an excellent chance that the sites that you visit are being recorded. News stories frequently report firings of people "caught" surfing non-work-related sites while on the job. E-mails and voice mail messages can be easily, and usually legally, scrutinized by employers.

In the past, there were practical limits on the ability of your supervisors to monitor you, but technology has changed the rules, adding to job stress. Feeling that you are constantly being watched is stressful because it keeps you constantly "on guard."

As a mid-level manager at a regional bank's headquarters, Chris sat down at his computer at the end of a particularly hectic day to surf the Net. All he could think about was getting away. He visited the Web pages of several beach resorts. He noticed one that said, "Natural Beach." He clicked the URL and found that it was a "clothing optional" resort. Realizing that he had landed on a nude beach Web site, he thought how funny it would be if he mailed the Web site address to a friend down the hall.

Two weeks later he received an e-mail from the vice president he reported to. The message was marked urgent and read, "Meet me at my office at 2 p.m. today."

Just as Chris sat down in his office, Mr. Krammer asked, "What's this I hear about you visiting nude Web sites?"

Chris explained that he was looking for beach resorts to visit on his vacation later this summer. He accidentally stumbled on the nude site.

Mr. Krammer asked, "If it was an accident why did you e-mail Jim White the address?"

You may not be able to avoid surveillance entirely, but you can reduce the stress it causes by cultivating habits that safeguard you from the kind of trap that Chris fell into:

- If you surf the Net at work, make sure that you visit only work-related sites.
- If you send e-mail jokes, assume that many more people than the original recipient will see it.
- When typing e-mails, choose your words carefully.

Transcending Tech Fear

Just keeping up to speed with the changes in communications and office technology is stressful for most of us. Learning how to use a new device or unfamiliar software program is time consuming at best and intimidating at worst. To cope with the stress, some people resist learning, while others try to fake it. Both strategies just compound the stress.

Most people require a quiet, uninterrupted environment to be able to learn complex material. However, many workers have to learn new computer programs on the fly in noisy rooms subject to frequent interruptions while keeping up with their regular workload.

You may feel intimidated by the amount of jargon that is used on your job. You may not know of the meaning of terms such as RAM, download, floppy, hacker, microprocessor, and multimedia. If that's your situation, chances are you are already feeling dismayed to see some co-workers easily adapt to the new technologies while you find yourself left in the dust. You also may hesitate to ask for help for fear of looking stupid.

If so, you aren't alone. An MCI study found that 59 percent of 1000 adults surveyed reported that they were frustrated by new technologies. Weil and Rosen estimate that between 85 percent and 90 percent of the population have difficulty embracing new technology. Yet, whatever you feel about the new technologies, the reality is that they are here to stay. They will become progressively more important to the workplace, not less. So, you'll have to learn to live with them.

Approach the new technologies positively and use them to make your work easier. If the thought of learning how to use the computer is a daunting task, approach it from a different angle. Try to break the ice by using the computer to play some games on your lunch hour. This will allow you to build a different association, a comfort association. Computers can be used for fun as well as work. Get involved in the technology decision making in your organization.

Try the following:

- Ask for help from co-workers and supervisors.
- Take a computer class.
- Ask for on-the-job training paid by your employer.
- Ask friends for their e-mail addresses and practice by corresponding with them.

Ten years ago the Department of Psychiatry at the Kaiser Permanente Medical Center where I work converted to a computer-based appointment schedule. Some of the doctors and other professionals resisted this change saying, "This gives me less control over my practice," or "I don't have the time to learn the system." Instead, they continued to use a parallel paper system, which resulted in double the work and confusion to boot. Once they finally did make the conversion they were delighted with the efficiency and the time they saved.

Dr. Muddler was one of the people who dug in his heels when new technology was introduced. He maintained that as a psychologist his only responsibility was to provide his patients with good care. When the voice-mail system was installed, he complained that his patients could leave long-winded messages for him. He preferred to keep any and all communication with his patients face to face. Then when the computer scheduling system was adopted he was the last to give up his separate schedule book, arguing that he was losing control of his own caseload. When his colleagues told him that they were actually finding the computer scheduling system more efficient than the old paper system, he thought they were just rationalizing.

After months of refusing to learn the computer scheduling and phone mail systems, his supervisor, Dr. Ready, paid him a visit. Dr. Ready asked, "Jim, are you having trouble learning the systems? I would be more then happy to teach you."

"No, I am fine. I can learn it when I have the time."

"Oh, I see. I just thought, well… the others seemed to have been adjusting well."

Dr. Muddler went home that night wondering if his resistance to the change was connected to a strong underlying feeling of intimidation.

The next morning he asked one of his colleagues if he had trouble learning and found he was not alone in his feelings of initial insecurity.

His colleague gladly agreed to teach him and soon Dr. Muddler was singing the new system's praises. He became involved in a department-wide committee screening new software to adopt. He soon found he was more computer savvy then he ever could have dreamed.

Think of the time and energy Dr. Muddler wasted resisting the change. Fortunately, he eventually rechanneled that energy into learning the new system.

Telecommuting with Less Stress

An estimated 60 million Americans work from home, and their numbers are growing. Studies of large companies have shown that telecommuting results in 15 percent more productivity and saves up to $6,000 per year, per worker in overhead costs. Working from your computer at home has many advantages. However, if you telecommute you need to make sure that you don't let your work life dominate your home life.

Studies have found that working from home raises productivity but reduces leisure time. Telecommuters have trouble drawing a boundary between their private life and their work life.

Becky, for example, found it difficult to separate her work and her chores around the house. She had been a telecommuter for six months before she realized that she was working harder than when she was at the office. Between sending e-mail and typing reports, she found herself rushing into the laundry room to toss a load into the washer. Sometimes she would take a break to vacuum the living room carpet. She found that she was losing her concentration and thinking too much about her household chores at work.

Once in the middle of a phone call to her boss she said, "Hold on Bill, I've got to move a load to the dryer."

When she returned to the phone he said, "Maybe I could send you to my house to do the laundry."

Becky laughed politely but felt quite embarrassed. She realized that she needed to draw a clear line between her work and her chores at home. She decided that no chores would be done until she "got off" work at 5 p.m. She also decided to dress for work as if she was going into the office. Soon she found herself much more efficient and less stressed.

Telecommuters also suffer from isolation and the feeling that there is a lack of support for their effort. If you are a telecommuter, it's important that you have weekly face-to-face contact with your peers. Visit the central office. Weil and Rosen recommend that telecommuting works best if you limit it to three days a week. Also try the following:

- Attend social functions at the office or go to lunch with peers from work.
- Schedule meetings at your home.
- Create an office away from the living quarters, in a separate room if possible.
- Wear business clothes during work hours and casual clothes when you are not working.
- Take frequent breaks and use the saved commuting time for a morning walk.

Juggling the Nanosecond

Tech stress increases because of the fast-paced nature of many jobs today. Most people have trouble focusing while juggling multiple tasks. Workers make numerous mistakes trying to keep up with the hectic pace at work.

If you are like millions of workers, you may feel that time is your enemy. You are assigned projects that need to be completed yesterday. Your anxiety rises with the passage of each nanosecond.

You may find yourself rushing to a meeting knowing that you are already 10 minutes late while wondering how you are going to juggle all of your projects, answer all the e-mail, and return your phone messages.

Your brain is not capable of this kind of multiple tasking. Though you may be able to check your e-mail while you talk on the phone and write a quick note, you probably make countless mistakes.

Slow down. When you write an e-mail letter don't do anything else at the same time. Make sure that you have enough time to devote to writing without distractions. Provide yourself with a buffer of time. Ask yourself, "Do I really have time for this now?"

How spread out are you? How scattered are your thoughts? Does your mind wander to the conversation you had at lunch even though you are trying to concentrate on the computer screen? If you feel spread out, scattered, and spend a great deal of time trying not to daydream, chances are that you are stretched beyond your limits.

Technology has transformed and even erased traditional time and personal boundaries for many employees. Some companies expect you to be on call 24 hours a day, seven days a week, 365 days a year. And, the truth is, some employees accept or even encourage this because it makes them feel indispensable. You think you must respond immediately by pager even while in the bathroom. If you carry a cell phone, even a walk to the deli during lunch hour can be interrupted by a call from your boss, a colleague, or a customer.

Blane exemplified one of those executives stretched beyond his limits and buried in a blizzard of e-mails, cell phone calls, and beeps from his pager. He tried to get the most of every nanosecond. He always made several phone calls in his car on the way to work each morning. Once in his office he checked his voice mail while scanning his e-mail. After a quick walk to his mailbox to check for snail mail he was off to his first meeting of the morning. As he took the elevator ride to the 20th floor he managed another phone call. He usually found the meeting hard to follow because of all the pagers and cell phones beeping and ringing.

Then prior to the next meeting he checked his phone mail and e-mail back at his office. He responded to five e-mails and managed to return one phone call but found himself frustrated because he was lost in a phone tree. By his 11 a.m. meeting he had a raging headache. Nevertheless, he thought that the videoconference went well. But as he tried to reflect on the meeting he found he had forgotten the outcome of the meeting. Had the senior vice president from Seattle argued for an increase in production or was it a decrease?

He walked to the bistro across the street to get a bite to eat for lunch. He noticed Bill from the accounting office just as his cell phone rang. He sat down with Bill while talking on his cell phone to Jason from the production department. Jason asked, "What's the word on the number of units?"

Blane said, "I'm not sure. I think the guy from Seattle said another 50,000 units."

As Blane hung up he noticed that Bill was shaking his head. "What's wrong?"

"We don't have the capital for another 50,000."

"We don't? I wonder why..."

Back at his desk he searched through the 25 e-mails that came in during lunch. Nothing from Seattle. He decided to call the vice president but could not remember his last name. He called the home office and after 10 minutes of wading through a phone tree he reached a live person. He asked to be connected to the vice president and left a phone mail message marking it as urgent. The phone rang and his 1:30 p.m. phone conference call began. He had trouble concentrating during the conference. He found himself worrying about the production number. Should he call Jason and tell him to hold off?

One of the conference voices broke through his thoughts and asked, "Blane are you there?"

All of the voices in the phone conference laughed. Then one of them said, "Okay, we will meet again the same time next week."

While walking to production later in the afternoon he received a call on his cell phone from the vice president's secretary. She asked, "What were you calling about?"

Though he was feeling embarrassed Blane asked again about production goals.

"Haven't you heard that we have ordered a pause in production?"

Blane felt humiliated. He went immediately to Jason in production and told him to stop. Jason rolled his eyes.

On his way home that night Blane found himself beginning to make another phone call. Then he asked himself, "Is this really necessary?" He turned his phone and pager off. When he arrived home he vowed that he would not check his e-mail on his home computer. As he sat in his hot tub he decided that he would maintain a much less frenetic pace. Although checking his e-mails and phone mail and using his cell phone were important, he decided to be far more selective in how he utilized these tools. It was time to prioritize.

What can you learn from Blane's frenzied existence? As you try to balance the needs of your employer with your own sanity, consider doing the following:

- Don't check your e-mail on impulse. Schedule specific times for these checks.
- Prioritize which e-mails you return.
- Turn off your cell phone and pager at lunch unless required to have them on.
- Allow yourself enough time to give thoughtful and coherent responses to letters received.
- After a day of interruptions turn off all pagers and cell phones for a break at home.
- Don't do more than one thing at a time when sending messages.

Many people carry their cell phones and pagers around with them when there is no requirement that they do so. It makes them feel important to get a call or be paged while standing in line at the cafeteria. They may not admit it, but it is really a way of showing off. If you are one of these people, turn it all off now. The possible gains from looking important have their costs.

The stress of being always available is no reward for the negligible positive attention you receive. It is probably more the case that people will be irritated with you for the noise pollution. Or, if you are driving in your car and accept cell phone calls, other drivers are not only irritated with you but also afraid of you. If you are trying to impress people, find some other way to do it.

Make sure that the new technologies work for you rather than against you. Don't waste your energy by being a peacock. Pace yourself. Don't let the new technologies push you faster than you can work.

CHAPTER 13

Super Stress

JOB STRESS IS DIFFICULT TO manage for line workers, but it is even more complicated for people who occupy supervisory positions. There is an old saying that it is "lonely at the top." This is particularly true for mid-management supervisors. For this reason, this entire chapter focuses on supervisory stress.

With the increasing work pressures that have come with consolidations, downsizing, and the drive for higher productivity, supervisors have been feeling considerable stress. It is well known in the field of industrial psychology that people in mid-management suffer the most amount of pressure within an organization. I have been in four mid-management positions and can personally attest that adjusting to the role of a supervisor is one in which I was minimally trained, despite being a psychologist. For millions of people, including me, it was on-the-job training.

A beginning supervisor has to learn how and how *not* to react to workers who need to be counseled about their performance or the way they are interacting with co-workers. Sometimes supervision requires mediation between opposing parties. Being a supervisor means being a role model, teacher, and referee.

Unfortunately, many people advance to supervisory positions for reasons that have little to do with their skills to manage people. Some are promoted to supervisor simply because they have seniority, are friends with upper management, or have exaggerated their skills during a good performance in an interview.

It has been my experience that some organizations are more prone than others to elevating workers into supervisory positions.

Many advance people who are not ready for the promotion to supervisory duties. As a result of inappropriate promotions these supervisors create more tension among subordinates.

Organizations with poor supervisors often place worker productivity as the sole focus of their organizational goals. Productivity needs to be balanced with concern about employees. Productivity is generally lower in organizations that ignore workers' needs than in organizations that promote a team approach and workers' health.

Shock Absorbers

Supervisors are under pressure, especially during this era of downsizing and corporate takeovers. They are asked to do more with less while simultaneously being acutely aware that at anytime their job may be eliminated. They know that they are the most expendable people in a company that is being reorganized.

If you are a supervisor, you probably know that you don't have the luxury to turn to many people for support and encouragement. If you are working in a company going through a period of takeover or downsizing, you may feel lonely and isolated. The competition with fellow supervisors for survival may add to feeling less inclined to look to your peers for support.

I have referred to mid-managers who work in companies that are going through organizational change as "shock absorbers." They are in the position of letting the line staff know of new and often unpopular changes within the organization.

Soon after I became chief psychologist in the mid-1990s, I had the unenviable job of telling all of the psychologists that their sick days would be eliminated. In the future, they would have to take vacation days when sick. Though I disagreed with the policy, I was put in a position to explain it. Many of the psychologists were so upset with cuts to their benefits that one of them joked, "Don't be surprised if you find your tires slashed."

Many years before, I was pressured to fire people; I refused. I endured added shock-absorber stress. In yet another position, I was faced with a subordinate who needed disciplinary action but managed to find cover in someone above me. Mid-management receives fire from all angles.

Many supervisors suffer more stress from their relationships with fellow supervisors than they do with the line staff. This stress often results from overly ambitious and competitive peers who aggressively step over or manipulate everyone around them on their way to the top. It is difficult to move out of their way without getting trapped.

If you are a supervisor and find the role of being a shock absorber, wearing on you, it is time to take a good look at your coping style. Aspects of your personality may needlessly add to your job stress. After you identify them, you will be in a better position to make appropriate changes.

The Personality of the Supervisor

Many supervisors don't understand that their personality can ripple through the unit and come back to them like a boomerang. If, for example, a supervisor is arrogant and boastful, the line staff will probably lose respect for that supervisor. If a unit of workers dislikes its supervisor, not only will there be tension between that supervisor and the staff, but there will be disharmony within the unit. In contrast, if the supervisor is congenial and humble, the line staff will probably not only respect him but the social climate will be much more harmonious.

Some supervisory styles are prescriptions for job stress. They invariably result in worker dissatisfaction and more pressure. The two most destructive styles are:

- **The Autocratic Style:** Here the supervisor is on a perpetual mission to assert his authority. Everything is centralized and he has the last word. Because he doesn't delegate authority, he carries the burden of being involved in every decision. Workers feel that he micromanages and treats them like mindless serfs. They resent him and he can't understand why.

- **The Laissez-Faire Supervisor:** Here the supervisor is a "hands-off" manager. He participates in little of what the workers are doing. When the workers look for direction, he has none to offer. When he is asked by upper management, "What is going on in your unit?" he can offer little information. Often workers run their own ship and are not held accountable for their work. Consequently, the laissez-faire supervisor runs the risk of feeling perpetually inadequate and as if he is an imposter, a supervisor in name only.

Although autocratic supervisors are highly critical and laissez-faire supervisors fail to provide constructive criticism when appropriate, both extremes engender conflict and job stress.

If employees feel that they have no voice and that their opinions are worthless in the eyes of a supervisor, they will have little respect for him. This autocratic "top-down" management style will engender resentment among the employees. Not only does it foster contempt for management, but supervisors who manage in this way operate in a vacuum. They afford themselves little chance of gaining from the insights of the people who are actually doing the work.

Alternatively, if you are a supervisor who invites the opinions of those you supervise, you will probably not only earn their respect but also foster high morale. Also, you *will* gain from the insights of those that are actually doing the work. In this way, there will be a "bubbling up" of new ideas rather then a dictating down of commands that may or may not be useful.

If you adopt an idea generated from line staff everyone wins. Make sure that you do *not* take credit for the idea; instead, praise both the person and the idea.

Many supervisors make the mistake of giving only negative criticism. They apparently think that negative criticism will keep the line workers on their toes and heighten their productivity. What these supervisors fail to recognize is that this approach fosters tension, acrimony, and dissent. The workers will perpetually anticipate criticism and feel unappreciated. If you use this supervisory style, you will destroy any sense of teamwork.

Ironically, supervisors who overstate their power lose it in the eyes of those they supervise; power is best understated. A supervisor who pounds his chest and demands allegiance from his subordinates will actually lose their respect. Those supervisors who are respected are those that *earn* the respect of their subordinates. Make sure that you do *not*:

- Treat people rudely, with insensitivity and callousness.
- Indiscriminately hold one person up to praise while neglecting others who perform equally well.

- Appear as if you will step over anyone to gain another rung on the ladder.
- Delegate tasks as punishment.

If you are seeking or occupying a management position because the power is seductive, take a step back and reevaluate your goals. Power is paradoxical. Those that don't think they have enough of it will never be satisfied; they are dogs chasing their own tails.

If you are a supervisor who chases power for its own sake, you may do so because you do not feel worthwhile. But rather than engendering a feeling of worth, power grabbing undermines your foundation of self-esteem. Because it never leads to a sense of satiation, you are stuck in a trap; you perpetually feel empty. The end result is that you feel stressed and your staff will not respect you.

If you cannot think of any other reason to be a supervisor than to gain power, it is time to resign. On the other hand, if you can identify a sense of a mission or meaning to your job, you will be able to defuse some of the job stress. Having a sense of meaning and purpose not only helps you transcend adversity, but it also motivates you to strive to get people to work together for a common purpose.

Praise your staff for its good work. Employees will feel appreciated and want to work harder. The positive approach will become contagious; they may praise one another for a job well done. The overall effect will be one of team building.

Respect can be earned by:
- Treating people fairly.
- Admitting when you are wrong.
- Asking subordinates for their input.
- Demonstrating that you are willing to roll up your sleeves and join in the effort.
- Sharing a vision and direction.
- Promoting camaraderie instead of divisiveness.

As a supervisor, even your most casual comments can come back and slap you in the face. You must maintain a higher level of vigilance over your interactions with people than you had experienced as a line staff person. As a supervisor, you are held to a higher level of scrutiny.

Not long ago, supervisors were not monitored for abuse of their employees. Now entire agencies, including the Federal Department of Equal Employment Occupational Commission (EEOC) and the National Labor Relations Board (NLRB), regularly investigate allegations of abuse of authority.

If you are a supervisor, you must maintain a very clear sense of your personal boundaries. Whereas you may have joked with co-workers more freely in the past as a line worker, you are now held to a more rigorous standard. You, as supervisor, are scrutinized more closely because your actions can be seen as abusing your power.

This heightened sense of cautiousness doesn't mean that you ought to distance yourself from those you supervise. Make sure that you maintain an "open-door" policy; otherwise, you will create a "regal" image that your staff will resent. Your open-door policy involves letting people know that you are always willing to discuss work-related issues. An open-door policy garners respect; a closed-door policy garners disdain.

Balancing the Stress of Supervision

Good supervisors feel less stress when they maintain a balance between control and lack of it. They let go of the illusion of having total control and don't hide from authority by letting workers do what they please.

Being a balanced supervisor means that you need to provide direction and support for your workers. Let employees know that they will be held accountable for their job performance. If you fail to tell a troubled employee that improvement is needed, the consequences of this failure will come back to haunt you. This trap is often experienced by the laissez-faire supervisor, who trades the short-term avoidance of conflict for the long-term agony of dealing with a troubled employee. It contrasts the autocratic supervision style of a manager who criticizes everything and as a result is not taken seriously when he points to critical areas that need improvement.

As a balanced supervisor, you are clear, direct, and honest; you do not overreact to the minor imperfections of your employees. In this way, you let your employees know that you accept their imperfections but expect them to do their best.

If you hold your employees up to the impossible standard of being perfect, you set yourself up to be constantly disappointed. If you ride your employees for their minor imperfections, you not only create an atmosphere of tension, but also set yourself up to be shaken by every misstep. Don't lose sight of your priorities and become sidetracked by the nuisance of pseudo-problems.

Minimize your stress level by paying very close attention to the talents of your employees. Those employees with talents in a particular area can be delegated tasks that will make them successful. Happy employees enrich the company. If you fail to take the time to examine the talents of your employees, you run the risk of managing people who are responsibile for tasks that are beyond their ability to perform.

You will experience less stress if you delegate responsibilities to those people who are capable and talented; they can share in the overall effort to manage a unit. By allowing the people you supervise to be in charge of specific oversight responsibilities, you can promote a collective ownership of accountability. Your workers will feel that they are included and you will feel less alone.

Many supervisors learn that failing to delegate responsibilities results in more work for them and less respect from their subordinates. Edward learned this lesson the hard way. Initially, he couldn't understand why his employees seemed to be so disrespectful toward him. As their supervisor for the past four years, he had worked hard to make them respect his position with the company. After he found a nasty letter implying he was a dictator, he wondered where he went wrong.

He thought, "Sure, I've made it clear that I didn't want any insubordination, but I've never publicly humiliated anyone." He tried to make sure that the lines of authority were clear after the company was taken over by a bigger computer company. He reminded himself, "I'm still a decent guy."

Edward decided to confide in George, one of his peers. "What's going on? I'm not a dictator!" Edward protested.

"I know that, but they don't," George said. Then he looked at Edward with a sly smile, "You don't let them see you in any other way. Why don't you allow them to make some decisions on their own?"

Edward shook his head, "Because when they blow it, the buck stops with me."

"But they will never learn anything, and they think you're treating them like children."

"Well, I just want to make sure that things are done right."

"Start delegating! What happens if you get sick? Who's going to rise to the occasion? You've got to start encouraging them to learn. Besides they'll appreciate it."

Edward thought long and hard about this advice. Finally, he decided to meet with some of his best employees. He made them team leaders and told them they could come to him with questions at anytime, but they didn't have to clear their decisions. They looked at him skeptically. He saw immediately that they didn't trust him, so he added, "Look, I know I have been a little overinvolved, but I think it is time to give you all some slack."

Over the next few weeks Edward was delighted to find that the line workers actually said hello to him, whereas before they had all ignored him. Eventually, he found himself breathing a sigh of relief; not only were people doing a good job, but soon they treated him as someone they wanted to spend time talking with in the lunchroom.

His subordinates responded positively, and Edward's workload eased considerably as a result of learning to delegate. If you find yourself having difficulty delegating, keep in mind what Edward gained by bolstering his relationships with co-workers and by getting help with the workload.

Whatever your predicament as a supervisor, strive for balance. Be honest, clear, and fair with your employees. This will allow you to cope with job stress and turn your job into a rewarding experience.

CHAPTER 14

Should You Take Time Off?

SOME PEOPLE EXPERIENCING JOB STRESS struggle with the question: "Should I take time off from work until I recover from the job stress?" The answer to this question should pose another one: "What am I going to do with the time off?" How you use your time off is critically important. Some people use the time productively and recover from the accumulated stress. Others use the time unproductively and fall into a black hole, becoming more depressed and anxious.

Avoiding the Black Hole

I have seen people who, by the time they get referred to me, have spent their time off work doing essentially nothing healthy. Most of them sat in their living room day after day watching television with the drapes closed. It is as if they have gone into hibernation hoping that a bad winter storm would pass.

You may feel that television provides you with a healthy escape from job stress. Think of it as a black hole; excessive television viewing compresses you into one blank frame of mind.

Do not sit in front the television because "there is nothing else to do." Excessive television viewing is analogous to sinking in quicksand; the more you watch, the more you will be tempted to watch. It is extremely addictive and can be thought of as "dead time." You should not live in dead time when you are recuperating.

Certainly, watching a select and limited number of television programs can be rewarding. But just as you do not eat ice cream all day long because it becomes less of a treat and a dietary disaster, excessive television viewing is emotionally malnourishing. You need emotional nourishment, not junk food for your mind.

When spending your time away from work, make sure you use it constructively. Don't sit around thinking about work. Many people spend their time off replaying in their minds the same work scenes. They retraumatize themselves each time they rehash the same conversations with their abusive supervisor or think about the mound of work waiting for them upon their return to work. They think about how they cannot possibly accomplish their tasks.

These replays have physiological and emotional consequences. The same stress hormones shoot through the body, the same neuropathways fire in the brain, almost as if one is deepening a scratch in a record. These replayed scenes groove one's mind and emotions into a rut. The emotional consequences of this rut exacerbate the symptoms of depression and anxiety. It is as if you brought the job home with you.

If you use your time off replaying the traumatic events experienced at work, then the time off is counterproductive. You should ask yourself, "If I am just reliving what I was experiencing at work, what is the point of being off work?" and "If this is all I am going to do when I am off work, maybe I ought to return to work. At least I will be getting paid for my stress."

Use your time off to refuel yourself, recuperate, and slow down. If you return to work emotionally exhausted, you will be less able to deal with the challenge of job stress. This will only result in bringing home more tension again.

You should be using the time off from work to dislodge yourself from job stress. By engaging in activities and pastimes that "change the subject" away from work, you will be able to invest your energies in stress reduction. Go to a concert or play. Take a workshop. Go fishing. Change your usual life pattern of "killing time" before returning to work.

For many people, music serves a therapeutic function; it is an outlet, a source of rejuvenation, and a soother. If you play a musical instrument, now is the time to pick it back up. Now is the time to use it to rejuvenate. Picking it up again will be like priming the pump and triggering a positive chain of events. You can get together with friends who also play instruments or simply become lost in playing a particular piece of music.

Even if you do not play an instrument you can replenish yourself by listening to music. An entire field of rehabilitation called music therapy was founded upon the principal that music can dislodge people from their "stuck" position and mobilize them into constructive activities.

Here is how it works: Listening to music is largely an emotional experience. Listening to a particular piece of music stirs your emotions and bypasses your critical thoughts. Because music resonates with "other" moods, you essentially change the mood just as if you are changing the subject. It is for this reason that you do not want to listen to abrasive and depressing music with negative lyrics. Listen to music that inspires, soothes, vitalizes or quiets your mind.

If art had been an important part of your life before experiencing job stress, now is the time to rekindle your interest. Though you do not feel like painting, drawing, or throwing pots, now is the time to push yourself to use these talents as therapy. Similar to music therapy, the field of art therapy has shown that artistic expression can be quite soothing. Even if you feel that you have little talent, you will still benefit from artistic expression. Buy some art materials, or take an art class.

If you engage in some form of exercise, you will not only gain from the physical benefit of exercise but also from feeling more confident. If you engage in a group sport such as baseball, volleyball, or basketball, you will gain from the social contact.

Make contact with people. Many people who experience job stress have so immersed themselves in their jobs that their social contacts only occur at work. When they feel overwhelmed with stress, these contacts become compromised. Social isolation results in more stress in the form of anxiety and depression. If you force yourself to socialize, you will be better able to cope with the feelings associated with job stress and mute feelings of anxiety and depression.

If you spent all your time at work and had few social contacts outside of that work environment, you may feel that the bridges have been burnt for social contact. You may feel that it is next to impossible to stir up the motivation to make new social contacts, and you may not know where to turn.

A structured activity may be a good place to start. A class or organized interest group could help you find the "safety" of as structured social activity, which is "safe" and nonthreatening because its focus is not specifically on meeting people. You will not need to extend yourself beyond your capability. If, for example, you were to enroll in an art class, you and your fellow students could focus on artwork and the social contact takes place on the side. A structured activity will allow you to socialize in a nonthreatening atmosphere.

You might think of social contact as a safety net, insuring that you will not fall more deeply into trouble and helping you bounce back into a healthier state of mind. Sally used the social safety net to bounce back into work with a new attitude.

It had been two months since her supervisor told her that she was not measuring up to his expectations. She had yet to complete the project he had assigned to her early in the year. The more she felt poorly about herself, the more she felt inadequate at work. Her energy level dropped and she began to withdraw from co-workers. Sally began to use up her sick days, and soon she was out on disability.

The office had been the center of her social life and she had few friends outside of work. Within a short period of time she found herself becoming more depressed. Her sister, Karen, became alarmed at the sudden change in Sally's loss of optimism. Karen had always looked up to Sally as a role model and inspiration. Sally's drive and ambition seemed to wither in front of her. Karen asked Sally to go on a Sierra Club hike on Saturday. "No, Karen I'm not up to it," Sally protested.

"That's the reason you should go. Once you get out there with us you will feel better."

"But I don't feel like being around people. I just can't put on a happy face," Sally replied.

"You don't have to talk with anyone. Just hike with us. Enjoy the view of the mountains."

Sally reluctantly agreed. During the hike she found herself slowly waking up as if from a bad dream. At the stop for lunch she found herself responding to her fellow hikers with more ease than she felt in weeks. By the end of the hike she, Karen, and the others were planning another hike for the next Saturday.

She decided to return to work. She felt less bogged down and more confident. She worked diligently, looking forward to the weekend and the next hike with her new friends. The following week she pushed herself to eat lunch with her co-workers. Soon she began to feel like her old self. She managed to ask for help, and a few weeks later the project was going well.

Had Sally said no to her sister and remained socially isolated, it is probable that her depression would have worsened. By getting out of the house and engaging in a structured social activity, she jarred herself out of the rut.

Disability and Workers' Compensation

You may be one of the millions of people who have applied for state disability payments or workers' compensation. Yet, you may not know that the workers' compensation system is a tangled and brutal obstacle course. If you apply for workers' compensation, you may assume that you will be awarded an automatic check. Nothing can be further from the truth. Even if you win your case, the amount awarded by workers' compensation does not make up for or equal the trouble of delaying everything else in your life.

During the past several years, the number of people applying for workers' compensation for stress claims rose dramatically. There was a 700 percent increase in workers' compensation cases in California during the past 10 years. As a vivid reflection of the staggering increase in claims, a judge was granted an award after he alleged that he had a stroke because of the job stress brought on by the increase in workers' compensation cases heard in his court.

In California, workers' compensation cost employers $1 billion in medical and legal fees. In many states, there is now a backlog in work-related stress cases. This means big delays in adjudication and compensation if your case is approved.

Against this backdrop, broad changes have taken place. The requirements for being approved have tightened considerably, but despite these new regulations, the number of applications has not decreased.

Prior to submitting your claim for workers' compensation, you have the right to maintain confidentiality for any mental health treatment you have received. This means that only by your written consent can your mental health provider release information regarding your treatment. Once you file for workers' compensation, you will have to waive your right to confidentiality. As a result of your claim, your employer's insurance carrier can have access to your mental health records.

When you apply for workers' compensation, your claim must be authorized by a claims examiner employed by your employer's insurance carrier before you can receive any benefits. From the very beginning of the process you are placed in an adversarial position with your employer. You must prove that your stress is due to work conditions. and *not* the result of lawful, nondiscriminatory, and good faith on that part of your employer. You must demonstrate *bad* faith on the part of your employer, not just that you experienced stress. People can experience stress from legitimate work assignments, but a claim based on this type of stress is *not* eligible for compensation. You must demonstrate that you were actually abused.

From most employers' points of view, as well as their insurance companies, it is not cost effective to award workers' compensation claims. They are concerned that if they allow you to be awarded a claim for stress, many more people will apply for workers' compensation because stress is quite common to work. The increase in payouts would result in increased insurance premiums for employers and a loss of money for the insurance companies.

Many employers oppose stress-related claims not only because of high costs but also because of suspicion that cases may be fabricated or exaggerated. In the past, California awarded approval for workers' compensation if the job stress accounted for 10 percent of the psychological problems a person experienced at the time of evaluation. Now the industrial injury must amount to 51 percent of the claimant's psychological problems. Arkansas now compensates workers for stress only when it is the result of a violent crimes. West Virginia and Oklahoma have excluded psychological injury altogether from their lists of conditions eligible for workers' compensation.

The insurance companies have orchestrated a well-organized defense against work-related stress claims. Because they essentially lose money in payouts, they have insured themselves against "nuisance claims." Their effort has been oriented toward contracting with psychiatrists and psychologists who may have a tendency to find that the claimant's stress is related to other causes—any other cause but the job itself. For this reason, many people refer to these doctors as "hired guns." I have seen numerous people apply for workers' compensation and be devastated by reading the hired gun's evaluation. For example, one woman read in a psychological report that she overreacted to her job situation because she had a poor relationship with her father when she was a child. After reading the report, she became more depressed.

It is not uncommon for workers to file claims for workers' compensation for stress, then wait out the process before deciding what they will do about moving on with their lives. Instead of looking for another job or enrolling in a retraining program, they may suffer the illusion that there is a pot of gold at the end of the rainbow.

I have seen numerous people who have applied for workers' compensation because they had convinced themselves that their weak case was in fact a good case. Some regard the amount of money they could potentially receive as a means to an early retirement. Similarly, it is very common to encounter people who want their state disability extended when in fact they are quite capable of working. Do not fall into this trap.

I am not suggesting that you should never apply for workers' compensation; you may have a perfectly justifiable case, and it may be advisable to apply. If you do pursue a claim and you are denied, there are still a few options left. If your workers' compensation claim is denied on the initial round, you can appeal the decision to the Workers' Compensation Appeals Board. At this point it is advisable to seek legal counsel; even upon appeal, a claim may be a long shot at best, and appeals may take up to two years to resolve. Many people contract the services of a workers' compensation attorney to help them through the appeal process; these attorneys are entitled to 12.5 percent of the total award if your appeal is successful.

Some people believe that they are punishing their company by filing a workers' compensation claim. If you feel that the treatment you received is not legally justified and you want your company held accountable, there are more direct means through which you can exercise your rights. For example:

- If you were harassed or discriminated against due to race, age, or sex, call the EEOC. A caseworker from the EEOC will interview you and determine if further investigation is warranted. If he feels that the case should be pursued, he will interview co-workers and management, then file a report.
- You can also contact your state's department of employment for personal as opposed to class harassment.

- If you want to resolve the issues of back pay or sick/vacation leave, call the NLRB. Staff at the NLRB will help resolve administrative and union-related issues.
- If you feel that your workplace is unsafe and that you have been injured as a result, call the federal or state Office of Safety Administration. They will send an investigator and if warranted will cite your company, requiring that it resolve the problems. If your company does not resolve the problems, it could be potentially be shut down.
- If you feel you have a legal case, especially if the above investigations are found in your favor, you can consult with an attorney.

A word of caution: I have seen patients who have spent thousands of dollars pursuing a case that their attorney had encouraged them to pursue. One method of determining if you do have a case that will not simply be a money drain is to find an attorney who will agree to be paid only if the case is won. Most attorneys will not pursue cases that they believe will not result in a high commission for themselves. On the other hand, attorneys will pursue cases if they are paid a retainer and the costs for any services rendered. They will get paid whether or not you have a good case. Therefore, I caution people to think twice about contracting with an attorney if they cannot find an attorney who will represent them without a retainer. However, if the EEOC or OSSA ruled in your favor, then perhaps you can be more confident.

Even if you do survive the workers' compensation appeal process and are awarded compensation, what do you receive?

- The system will pay for treatment until you have recovered enough to be able to return to work.
- If for some reason you cannot recover sufficiently to return to either your previous job or modified work, vocational rehabilitation services may be provided for retraining so that you can perform another line of work.
- During the time that you are off work receiving treatment and/or vocational rehabilitation, you will be given a percentage of your average weekly pay.

Sam felt stuck in his position because he expected the workers' compensation system to resolve his job stress. It all started when his new supervisor, Blake, transferred into the warehouse. He knew that his 10 years with the company were in jeopardy. He and his fellow warehouseman had been a tight group, but Blake began immediately to play favorites and marginalize those he did not like. It all seemed so arbitrary to Sam. When he found that he was not one of Blake's favorites he began to wonder why. He approached Blake and asked, "Is there something I'm doing or not doing?"

Blake responded immediately, "Yes. You seem to drag the rest of the crew down. Can you be a little more organized and move more quickly?"

Sam thought he worked no differently than his peers. He responded defensively, "How am I any different from Frank or Fred?"

"Fred and Frank don't hang around the soda machine for half an hour. They look for work. You slug along."

Within a week, Sam was second-guessing himself. He began to make mistakes and soon began to have mild panic attacks. He then found it hard to go to work; finally, he didn't return at all. He called the personnel department and asked what he should do about his absence. They gave him no answers, but asked if he was going to apply for workers' compensation. He immediately responded by saying yes. He felt that he had it coming to him; the company had hired Blake and now they should pay.

He left his house only to go to the grocery store. The drapes were drawn and he kept the television on for 24 hours a day. Sam sunk further into depression. His appetite and sleep became erratic. He thought about Blake almost continually, going over every conversation repeatedly. Because he had few social contacts outside of work, he had no way of determining if his "insights" made any sense.

Two weeks turned into two months. He felt convinced that workers' compensation was the only way to resolve his problem. But he was less confident after he was interviewed by the psychiatrist contracted by the insurance company. He managed to get a copy of the report and was horrified to read that the psychiatrist argued that his problem with Blake stemmed from his problem with his alcoholic father. He plunged further into depression. Now he knew he was trapped. He was convinced that if he returned to work he would eventually be fired. There seemed no way to punish Blake. He thought about filing an appeal, but even that seemed hopeless.

Then it dawned on him that he could look for another job. He put together a resume and hit the pavement. Just being out of the house made him feel a little better. After a few weeks he began to get some nibbles. He went out on a few interviews. On the third week he was relieved to hear that he could begin work immediately.

Is It Time to Move On?

Many people who experience job stress and know conditions will not change do not make an effort to leave. If you are one of them, you may lose a valuable chance to move on with your life. It is as if you are locked into one option—staying and suffering. While it is true that some people do have few options, you may underestimate your alternatives. You may be a person who feels trapped because you are convinced that the job options are limited "out there." Or you may feel that you are currently earning a salary that would be hard to replicate outside of your current position.

Whatever your particular reason for feeling stuck, you may want to consider the following questions:

- Have you really explored all of your job options by actually doing a job search? Have you even applied to any positions? Doing this alone may give you not only a different perspective, but also result in finding another job.
- Have you explored the possibly of a transfer within your company to another assignment or shift?
- Have you thoroughly talked to management and explored the possibly of a temporary change in assignment?
- If you feel or even know that you cannot receive the same pay in a different job, have you considered that the "cost" of staying is actually greater in terms of stress.
- Perhaps you are at risk of losing the job anyway? Leaving by quitting is more practical and looks better on your resume than being fired.
- Do you feel that you are locked into the job because of trying to maintain a particular lifestyle? Perhaps you can change your lifestyle; sell the vehicle with the expensive payments, eat out less. Lifestyle compromises will yield you greater rewards in the long run.

- You may feel locked into your job because you are vested in the retirement system in your company and do not want to start over. Perhaps there are some options you have not considered yet. Some people have chosen for early retirement; although they will receive a smaller check than they would have had if they stayed longer, that check can supplement the salary of another job. In time you will be vested in the new job and upon retirement receive an additional retirement check.

- You may try to work with your human resources or personnel department to explore how you can get a transfer, even if it means a demotion, to stay in the same system while you play out the clock to retirement. Perhaps the few dollars less you may receive could yield a higher gain by less stress.

Get to know what your company's resources have to offer in support. Most companies have either an on-staff or a contract employee assistance professional (EAP). Such counselors provide short-term counseling, usually up to five sessions.

Many people mistakenly believe that the counselor is an agent of the company and will give away their right to confidentiality, but an EAP counselor has to abide by the same confidentiality laws to which all mental health professionals are bound. Further, the EAP counselor, especially if she works for the employer, can provide you with valuable insight into the personnel practices of the company. In other words, if you are worried about possible disciplinary action against you, the EAP counselor can help clarify how the company could proceed with your case. Thus, you will be able to make an informed decision about what to do next.

If you have been off work and have received all the help that was available, your transition back to the job may still feel overwhelming. Most people feel more anxious just before returning to work than they do one week after being back on the job. This is because "anticipatory anxiety" is often worse than the anxiety you experience once you are back on the job. With anticipatory anxiety, you may anticipate the worst possible job stress upon your return. But often the worst-case scenario does not happen when you return to work; most people slowly acclimate to the work situation. But if a return to work results in more job stress after a few weeks of attempted acclimation, then it is advisable to move on and look for another job.

It is a given that looking for another job can be a very stressful experience. You may ask, "Why do I want to put myself through more stress?" If you get rejected by potential employers, you may feel personally rejected and further deflated. However, there is more to gain and less to lose than you may think. Consider your job search as:

- An important exploratory move that gives you exposure to the labor market.
- An opportunity to sharpen your interviewing skills.
- An opportunity for exposure to employers.

By looking for another job you afford yourself a broader perspective than if you were to sit back and wait for your dilemma with your current job to pass. This new perspective will probably include the belief that you actually have nothing to lose but everything to gain by looking for another job. The worst case scenario is that you may not find a job for a while.

For every position, there are more applicants than openings. That means that everyone but the one hired will be rejected. If you inoculate yourself with the belief that it will take time to find a job, then when the rejections come you will not be shocked and debilitated, but still ready to proceed with the job search.

A useful and productive way to look at this period is as an important pivotal point in your life. You do not have to stay in the same place. In fact, if you stay in the same place, you will invariably feel worse than you already do. Use the feelings you have now and the current situation as the impetus to make significant changes in your life. Ask yourself, "What can I do differently? How can I set different goals for myself that I can live with and feel good about?"

It is a good idea to take the following steps in developing your stress reduction and job transition program:

1. Do a thorough inventory of how stress has been reflected in your body. (That is, are your shoulders tense, do you have a queasy stomach?).
2. Identify the course of stress that you now may feel peaking. When did it begin and what factors contributed to it?
3. Find and structure in time in your day away from those stresses; allow for "down time" and practice some of the stress reduction techniques outlined in this book.

4. Use the time off from work to learn how to enjoy productive activities.

5. Do a thorough inventory of your personal goals for your future.

6. Consider taking steps to look for other jobs or training programs.

CHAPTER 15

Job Fishing

LOOKING FOR A JOB CAN be as difficult as working in a stressful position. Not only can a job search be a long, exhausting process that can challenge your patience, but it can also serve as a lesson in humility. Most successful job searches involve several rejections before you get a strike or even a nibble.

Because looking for work can be so exhausting, you must pace yourself. Many people assign themselves specific hours to look for work and schedule in enjoyable activities. For example, you might look for work from 9 a.m. to 2 p.m. daily, and then plan enjoyable and productive activities in the afternoon. You may go to the gym on Monday, Wednesday, and Friday, and take a class on Tuesday and Thursday. Whatever you do in your "off" hours, try to maintain a variety of activities.

Maintaining an active social life is critical while looking for work. Your job search can seem like a lonely experience, and it may seem to you that everyone is working but you. By maintaining a healthy social support system, you can prevent isolation and loneliness.

The Big Net

Your job search will be most successful if you throw a big net. If you are too selective in the type of position you are willing to target, then your wait may be interminably long. If you are trying to build a work history that will enable you to get the job of your dreams, you will have to work in some entry-level positions first.

Don't limit your job search to using one particular method. There are a variety of ways to go fishing for a job. Check the following sources:

- Newspapers.
- Internet sites.
- Headhunters.
- Word-of-mouth.
- Cold calls.
- Professional journals.
- Trade magazines.
- State and federal job listing boards.
- Unemployment offices.

You will need to build a resume that will open doors and catch the attention of those reading it without limiting you to one specific job type. On the other hand, you must not be so general that the reader will lose sight of your unique talents.

Most resumes include a section on qualifications and background, such as work history. Some include an objective section, which states the type of job you are seeking. If you use this method, you will probably have to modify the objective section for each job category you are targeting. If you are looking for a variety of positions and have a diverse background, develop a few resumes. One resume can highlight one set of talents while another can highlight a different set of talents.

If you are fortunate to have received awards, list them. List any professional organization or trade organization in which you are a member. Make sure that your resume is:

- Clear, to the point, pithy, and directed to the most important facts about your work history.
- Date specific, including months.
- Typo, grammar, spelling error free.

There are several mistakes people make when composing their resumes. Make sure that you do *not* write a resume that is:

- Long-winded.
- A misrepresentation of your background.
- Vague.
- Hastily written.
- Fraught with inaccurate dates.

Any of these mistakes will come back to haunt you. For example, if you misrepresent your background by either exaggeration or outright lying, at some point in the future someone will find out the truth. Some people have actually been prosecuted for such misrepresentations.

If your resume is vague, fluffy, and peppered with nebulous dates, the reader will probably be annoyed and wonder if you are a reflection of your resume. If you are trying to cover up a spotty work history or lack or experience, your scam will be obvious during the interview.

If you are now looking for work after a period of job stress or as the result of being laid off, chances are the thought of searching for a job seems overwhelming. You may want to enroll yourself in a job search class, which will provide you with guidance and support to structure your search.

Michael found that a structured job search program is just what he needed. He felt devastated after he was laid off from his job at the tractor factory. He had worked at the factory since he was 18 years old. The thought of hitting the pavement was so overwhelming that he sat out the first week of unemployment. His wife became nervous and said, "Don't you think you ought to look? We're not going to make the mortgage payment."

Michael didn't know where to begin. He went to file for unemployment. To his surprise there was a class called "Job Club" that taught job search techniques; it met every afternoon. Michael began attending the class and soon learned about how to use the Internet, search the newspapers, and make cold calls. Within a few weeks he got his first nibble. Then he found himself at a series of interviews. After six weeks of concerted effort he landed a job.

Don't hesitate to use whatever resources are available to you. As Michael did, you may find that structured support from a program may keep you on track and focused.

The Interview

When you reach the interview stage of your job search, you will have an opportunity to explain why you are the best choice for the job. But you can't just go in and argue that you are the one they should choose. You will have to prepare for the interview.

Prior to the interview, make sure that you know something about the company and how the job differs from other jobs of its type in other companies. In this way you come into the interview with a greater knowledge base than some of the other candidates for the same position whom come into the interview cold. Also, by doing this prior research you will be able to better compete with some of the candidates within company who are trying to move up.

Your prior knowledge will help you formulate questions to ask at the end of the interview, which will demonstrate that you are interested in the fine nuances of the operation of the company. Those interviewing you will probably be impressed with you initiative and depth.

Prior to the interview reflect on the reasons you want the job and be prepared to explain them convincingly. Try to match those reasons with the skills that the job will demand. If, for example, the position is a sales job and you have little sales experience, highlight your desire to work with people. Practice your sales ability by selling yourself persuasively with friends prior to the interview.

Always arrive early for an interview. Your punctuality will be noted and you will demonstrate that you are conscientious. Also, by arriving early you will allow yourself time to catch your breath and relax before the interview begins.

When you go out on an interview, be prepared for uncertain circumstances that have little to do with the interview itself. If you plan for potential problems then you will not have to enter the interview preoccupied. Prepare by doing the following:

- Bring an extra few copies of your resume and letters of recommendation in case the people interviewing you do not have one on hand.
- Leave with much more than enough time to arrive at the interview with a comfortable buffer.
- Bring a comb/brush and breath mints in case you have to freshen up.
- Drive to the interview site the day before to insure that you know where you are going.
- Make sure that they know how to contact you and that you will be able to respond immediately.

During the interview, you don't criticize your former employer. These comments will not only come back to haunt you, but those people who are interviewing you will wonder if you are a problem employee. They know that most people put their best foot forward during an interview. But if gossip and slander demonstrate your best foot, they will probably not want to be your next victims. If for some reason you are compelled to say that you didn't get along with someone, make sure that you are tactful and understate your opinion. They will fill in the rest.

If you are asked confusing questions, make sure that you ask for clarification. Do not answer impulsively, because you may not know what you are answering. Once you receive clarification, pause and reflect on what you think may be the most complete answer. Don't assume that the interviewer will understand cryptic attempts to hide your lack of knowledge.

Watch your body language. Make sure that you don't communicate defensiveness by folding your arms on your chest or tapping your foot. You need to demonstrate that you are open, relaxed, and alert. If you cross your legs or fold your arms, keep them in one position for a comfortable period of time before recrossing them or folding them again.

Watch the body language of the interviewers. If one of them appears aloof or disinterested, try to engage him with eye contact. If they collectively appear to be fidgeting and look like they want the interview to end, change your approach and highlight areas that have not been covered.

During the interview, don't:

- Swear or use slang.
- Chew gum or smoke.
- Act as though they should be honored to interview you.
- Focus on just one of the interviewers and ignore the others.

If you are asked an illegal or ethically compromised question such as your political affiliation or dating history, try to be tactful and be general. For example, if you are single and they ask if you date say, "Yes, I get out of the house some and take a variety of classes." Or perhaps, "I'm married." Don't elaborate.

Use light humor during the interview to break the tension and illustrate that you can be easygoing and relaxed, but make sure that your humor is not at the expense of anyone and cannot be viewed as in poor taste.

Be polite and personable during the interview. Try to make eye contact with everyone. If the interviewers introduce themselves by their first names, refer to them by those names at the end of the interview while you shake each of their hands.

At the end of the interview, restate your interest and say, "Now that I have heard more about your company, I'm even more interested and excited about the possibility of working here with you." Thank them for the opportunity to interview with their company.

You may want to make a few notes after the interview of points you forgot to make; then send a thank you letter that adds those points. This letter will serve two functions. Most importantly, it will keep your presence alive in their minds. Also it will demonstrate that you are so conscientious that you have thought about intricate details of the interview long after it has past.

Brad seemed to do all the wrong things during an interview. Unfortunately, he had no idea how badly he appeared to the people interviewing him. He thought that because he had a strong resume and had always been able to write good introductory letters, his qualifications should shine through his gruff exterior. But when it came to the interview, he unknowingly irritated the interviewers. He was fond of asking the interviewers "Tell me why I should want to work here." Usually, he found that their eyes glazed over, a sign he thought reflected their inability to put forth a good argument.

Then, everything changed when on his sixth interview. One of the people said, "Let me get this straight. Are you trying to turn the table on us? Does this means that arrogance is one of your attributes?" Brad didn't know what to do. He completely reexamined his approach to interviewing. He decided that the gum he had chewed had to go and so did his practice of showing up "fashionably late." He bought a few books on how to interview and learned how to make eye contact, watch body language, and humbly ask for clarification on questions that seemed ambiguous. After the next interview, he was delighted to hear that he made it as one of the finalists. He knew he was on the right track.

Don't exude arrogance, as Brad did. Program yourself for your next interview by giving serious thought to the points made in this chapter. Most of all, practice your interviewing skills. Ask your spouse or friend to give you feedback on your style and presentation. Consider each interview as a learning experience. Don't be discouraged if you are not hired right away. There is always another opportunity around the corner.

CHAPTER 16

Making an Attitude Adjustment

PART OF YOUR JOB STRESS may be the result of your attitude. You may respond to every interaction with co-workers with such seriousness that any imperfection is sign of ill intent. You may be unable to lighten up and use humor. Or you may manage your time so badly that you have no room to breathe.

Some people who experience job stress have trouble differentiating themselves from their jobs. If so, personal boundaries are confused with the boundaries of the job. Try to remember that you are **not** your job. One essential way to insure that you have not fused yourself seamlessly with your job is to maintain a rich and varied life outside your work. If there is nothing in your life but work, there is no time off.

On the weekends and evenings you should engage in activities that vitalize, soothe, and capture your attention. If on the other hand you simply "kill time" until you return to work, you will invariably think about work while you are supposedly recuperating from it. But if you are thoroughly involved in hobbies, intellectual pursuits, sports, entertainment, and time with family, your time off can be rejuvenating. By making your life as broad as you can, your time off from the job will be what you need to distance yourself more effectively from stress.

Manage Your Time

Because stress can be increased just by the experience of rushing from task to task, time management is an important part of stress reduction. It is especially the case if you are a "rushaholic," who always needs to be somewhere 10 minutes ago. You will need to shift into a lower gear. Slowing down will actually allow you to get more done because your mind will not be as scattered. You will be more able to focus on what you are doing when you are doing it.

Time management will require that you:

- Prioritize the important tasks.
- Work out a schedule that will focus on the most important tasks first.
- Allow yourself enough time to complete each task with breathing room to collect yourself before moving on to the next task.
- Delegate tasks to others who can help. Do not excuse yourself by saying, "They won't do it right," and "I will need to do it so that it will get done."
- Do your best at each task and allow yourself to be human.

Stress Tolerance

Some people refer to themselves as "perfectionists." Generally, they set unrealistically high standards and feel inadequate if they do not live up to them. These standards are often impossible to meet. A "perfectionist" essentially sets himself up for a no-win situation, because he continually finds out that he is not perfect. Perfectionists actually do not feel perfect inside; they often try to overcompensate for feeling anxious by being "over perfect" on the outside. Being a perfectionist is not a good strategy to deal with job stress. Your stress will increase because perfectionism is unattainable.

It is not uncommon for perfectionists to try to accomplish something and then feel overwhelmed because they have no control. It is always good to keep in mind a saying, that 12-Step members refer to as the "Serenity Prayer":

God grant me the serenity to accept the things I cannot change,
Courage to change those things I can,
And the wisdom to know the difference.

Suzanne Kobassa and Salvator Maddi, two research psychologists from the University of Chicago, identified personality characteristics that help a person deal with stress. They studied busy executives and identified three characteristics they had in common:

- **Commitment**: The person felt invested in what he was doing and showed energy and interest in his duties.
- **Control**: The executives had a realistic sense that what they were doing is in the realm of control, that is, they felt they were active participants in their work instead of feeling hopeless victims of the work conditions.
- **Challenge**: They view change as an opportunity to act rather than a crisis to defend against.

The researchers found that these "Big Three" factors help people stay healthy despite dealing with high amounts of stress. They referred to these three factors as essential characteristics of "stress hardy" individuals. Stress hardy people are able to deal with stress that many people find unbearable.

As you cultivate stress hardiness, keep in mind that you still need the support of friends and family members. Kobassa found that stress hardy people have the capacity to tap into social support, which helps them blunt the impact of stressful events. Kobassa was careful to point out that the social support must be directed toward caring and encouragement, rather than fostering self-pity and dependence, and helping you explore your options.

Most people benefit from the belief that their job is leading them somewhere. Just as the belief in being stagnant in a "dead-end job" leads to stress, the opposite belief leads to interest and potential enthusiasm. The lack of the opportunity for promotion or job enrichment can be as destructive as the lack of job security. But, just as under-promotion can lead to stress, so can over-promotion. You should strive for a balance.

Professor Mihaly Csikszentmihalyi of the University of Chicago has described how people can avoid being overwhelmed with anxiety while at the same time as avoiding boredom. If a person invests his energy to find balance between being overwhelmed with stimulation and anxiety on the one hand and boredom on the other hand, he can experience flow—meaning enjoyment.

Your sense of enjoyment will increase if you also develop a sense of optimism and ambition. Dr. Daniel Goldman drew attention to the importance of optimism and ambition as being characteristics of "emotional intelligence." These two characteristics can be cultivated and expanded upon to provide you the perspective and direction to approach a bright future.

Optimism is more than seeing the glass half full. Cultivating an optimistic perspective may seem a broad jump while you are experiencing a high degree of job stress. You may think that there is nothing to feel optimistic about. However, a sense of optimism will emerge if you look past your current situation and focus on "possibilities" and "potentialities." Doing this will require unlocking yourself from the frame that you and your job are one. As noted earlier, you have to see yourself as larger than your job. By focusing on what you want to happen, you can see a potential light at the end of the tunnel.

You need the emotional fuel and the drive to make these possibilities an actuality. This is where ambition comes into play. Healthy ambition is *not* aggressiveness. It does not involve stepping over of other people to attain one's goals. Healthy ambition is the assertiveness and goal-driven sense of purpose that can give your life meaning.

If you once dreamed of being a teacher but got diverted because of having to raise children, use this period of job stress to rekindle that dream. Make an attempt to view this possibility as a potential future. If you feel that your goals are not possible in your current position or within your current company, then use this stressful period to move into an environment that has the potential you need.

If you make these attitude changes, you will be free to deal effectively with job stress. On the other hand, if you fail to make these changes your job stress will be exaggerated and seemingly insurmountable.

George is a person whose job stress was intensified by his poor attitude. He prided himself in his cynicism, often arguing that it was actually "realism." He held a computer support job for seven years despite often telling co-workers that the company was "abusive" and "not a friend of the people who really do the work."

One day his co-workers, Peter asked, "Hey, if you hate it around here so much why don't you look for another job?"

"I'm thinking about it," George snapped back.

Jim, another co-worker, overheard the two talking and he laughed. "George, you've been saying you're going to look for another job for years."

George couldn't get Jim's comment out of his mind as he drove home that evening. He realized that he had complained for years and hadn't done anything about it. Then it occurred to him that at his previous job he had a reputation as a pessimist. Back then he complained about that company too. He realized that he had been unhappy with his jobs as far back as he could remember. He had spent an inordinate amount of time complaining and not enough time doing anything about what he complained about. He knew that management saw him as an agitator. But he had until that moment thought of himself as the "conscience" of the company.

By the time he pulled into his driveway he wasn't so sure that his pessimism was really an asset. For the next several days he found himself wondering if his pessimism had contributed to job stress.

Don't behave as George did and make yourself and those around you miserable because of a negative attitude. Think twice before you call yourself a "realist."

CHAPTER 17

Get Some Sleep

IF YOU ARE EXPERIENCING JOB stress, you are probably also having sleep problems. When you feel tense, it is understandably difficult to unwind and sleep. Stress hormones do not decrease at night. Stress raises the levels of the neurotransmitters norepinephrine and epinephrine, and both of these neurotransmitters activate your nervous system. You may keep yourself charged up and tense by thinking about what is happening at work and what you have waiting for you the next day.

Insomnia is very common. Many surveys have shown that as many as 95 percent of people report that they have had insomnia at least once in their lives. Approximately 50 percent of people report that they have trouble sleeping once a week and 15 percent of people report that they have had trouble sleeping two nights a week.

You would think because insomnia is reported to be such a widespread problem that physicians would be prepared to help. But most physicians are not well trained in sleep studies. In a congressionally funded study, Dr. William Dement of Stanford University found that most physicians receive just 40 minutes of training in sleep study in all of their years of education. This void in training is reflected in their treatment of patients. Of millions of medical records surveyed, there were no reports of insomnia. It was found that 95 percent of sleep problems go undiagnosed. Physicians do not usually ask about insomnia. When they hear complaints from their patients about insomnia they typically prescribe benzodiazepines, despite the fact that most medical journals recommend a non-drug approach to insomnia. In fact, $100 million annually are spent on drug treatment of insomnia.

Because sleep problems are so common with people experiencing job stress and the medical help is so sparse, this chapter is devoted entirely to sleep. It focuses on the factors that affect sleep and how you can insure that you can maximize the quality of your sleep time.

Sleep: What It Is and What It Is Not

Sleep has been studied extensively for more than 70 years; there are approximately 400 sleep labs in the United States. Since the 1930s, researchers have been able to identify the types and the stages of sleep. There are three types of sleep: slow wave, fast wave, and dream sleep.

In dream sleep, your eyes move; thus, dream researchers referred to this type of sleep as Rapid Eye Movement (REM) sleep. Although we generally go through REM periods every 90 minutes, most of REM is packed into the latter portion of our sleep cycle. In contrast, the slowest wave sleep occurs earlier in the sleep cycle. The chart on the facing page illustrates a typical night of sleep.

Stage 1 is a transition state between waking and sleeping. The brain waves are fast and if awakened from this stage of sleep, most people will report that they were not really asleep.

In Stage 2, sleep is light and the brain waves are referred to as theta waves. Many insomnia patients complain that they do not sleep when in fact they are experiencing Stage 2 sleep. We spend half of the night in Stage 2 sleep, which increases during periods of stress.

Stages 3 and 4 are considered deep sleep, when we produce slow brain waves, referred to as delta waves. This is the most important stage of sleep. It is here that your immune system gets a boost. Body functions slow down. If you are deprived of deep sleep your immune system will be suppressed and your body may ache. However, because stress increases the activating neurotransmitters norepinephrine and epinephrine, it also results in a decrease in slow wave sleep. Fortunately, if you are sleep deprived, the first stage to rebound is deep sleep.

When research subjects were awakened during dream sleep, they reported vivid visual dreams. Most body functions appear to be much like wakefulness. Metabolism is up during REM sleep and energizing neurotransmitters are active. REM sleep is called "paradoxical sleep" for this reason. You may dream that you are running and most of

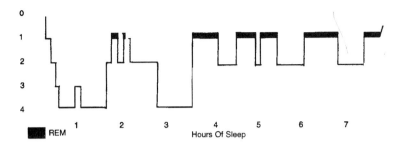

~~		Awake
~~		REM
~~		Stage 2
~~		Stage 3
~~		Stage 4

Chart 17.1. Stages of sleep

your organs function as if you are running. The only difference is that you are dreaming and your limbs are paralyzed. People who are depressed often experience "early morning awakening." When they wake up in the early morning, it is during REM sleep.

Overall sleep is very much tied to the light of the day and the dark of night. Light is taken in through your eyes, and your retina sends the information to your pineal gland, which is positioned in the middle of your brain. Your pineal gland will suppress the production of melatonin, thereby convincing the brain that it is daytime and not time to become sedated. In contrast, when it is dark outside your retina sends information to your pineal gland that it is night outside and it should produce melatonin to induce sedation.

BODY TEMPERATURE

(°C)

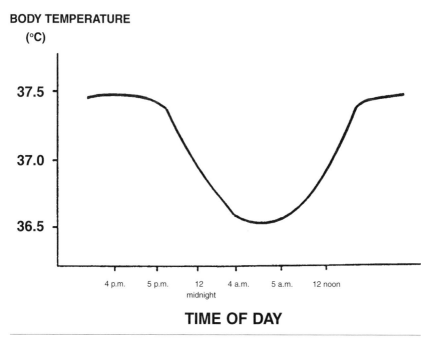

TIME OF DAY

Chart 17.2. Body temperature cycle

Your circadian rhythm is not only tied to the exposure to light but also to body temperature. Ideally, when you go to sleep at night your body temperature is dropping. Just before you wake up your body temperature is on the rise. When you get out of bed, the exposure to light and movement of your body promote a rise in body temperature. A typical body temperature cycle is pictured in the chart above.

Insomnia patients have difficulty with the regulation of their body temperature. Some insomnia patients cause their body temperature to increase at night, when it should be going down, by getting less physical activity in the daytime. By not exercising during the day, they promote less of a dip in body temperature in the night.

To correct these problems, keep your room cool during bedtime and exercise. When you get up in the morning, make sure that you are exposed to the normal amount of light so that your body can adjust to the correct body temperature cycle.

Most people feel worse just as they wake up after being deprived sleep. As your body temperature rises, you are exposed to light, and you move around, you will feel better. However, the way that you think about your sleep deprivation will affect how you will feel the rest of the day. If you think the loss of sleep is a major problem, the result will be a dampened mood and you will feel worse.

There have been numerous studies on the effect of sleep loss. Because most of sleep research takes place in universities, we know a lot about the cost of sleep deprivation on college students. It has been shown that college students who are sleep deprived but at least have managed 5 1/2 hours of sleep at night suffer no major problems with thinking ability. However, once they get less than 5 1/2 hours of sleep, thinking ability drops, as measured by performance on psychological tests.

Support for the 5 1/2-hour concept comes from an unlikely source. A prominent sleep researcher who also happens to be an avid sailboat racer assessed the performance of around-the-world racers. He found that those sailors who slept less than 5 1/2 hours also placed poorly in the race, because they made navigational mistakes. However, if a racer got more than 5 1/2 hours they also placed poorly, because they were not awake to make important navigational changes. He found that racers who managed just 5 1/2 hours of sleep placed best in the race.

It appears that 5 1/2 hours of sleep represents what most researchers regard as what our bodies need at the very least. For this reason, 5 1/2 hours is referred to as the "core sleep." It is during core sleep that you receive all of your nightly slow wave sleep and 50 percent of your REM sleep. Despite losing 50 percent of your REM sleep, you will lose the expendable light sleep, the fast wave light sleep. Therefore, you need not be overly concerned about insomnia if you are getting at least 5 1/2 hours of sleep—your core sleep.

Make sure that your attitude about sleep loss doesn't contribute to more stress. Karen fell into this trap. She began to lose sleep as soon as a new supervisor was transferred into her unit. As a Medicaid eligibility worker for the county she had already felt stressed because of the rapidly changing guidelines to determine eligibility. The new supervisor announced that she would audit 10 cases from each worker.

Karen had always tried to maintain a strict eight hours of sleep per night. But now she was consistently losing two hours of sleep each night. She began to worry that she would make mistakes because of her sleep loss.

She told her co-worker, Susan, that she expected to "get caught with big mistakes" during the audit. As Karen worried each day she found that indeed she was making mistakes and later that night she tossed and turned, losing sleep.

She enrolled in a sleep seminar and learned that she still had maintained her core sleep. Soon she didn't worry about mistakes and found that she made less of them. To her delight, her sleep improved steadily over the next week.

As Karen did, you can avoid needless worry about a few hours of sleep loss. But if you begin to lose some of your core sleep on a consistent basis, your insomnia will have to be dealt with by using a different strategy.

Insomnia

Insomnia is a major problem for most people who are experiencing job stress. There are two types of insomnia: early insomnia and sleep maintenance insomnia. If you have early insomnia you have difficulty getting to sleep. If you have sleep maintenance insomnia, you have difficulty staying asleep. With sleep maintenance insomnia you may fall asleep without difficulty but you wake up in the middle of the night and have trouble getting back to sleep. Early insomnia and sleep maintenance insomnia are both characterized by at least 1 to 1 1/2 hours of sleeplessness while lying in bed.

But, keep in mind that many people overestimate the time that it takes for them to get to sleep. If you are stressed, even a little time awake will feel like hours. Albert Einstein once described relativity this way: "If you are with a lover, a minute feels like a second. But if you are in pain a minute feels like an hour." If you are troubled by not being able to sleep you will probably overestimate the time you went without sleep. On the other hand, when was the last time you complained that you lost sleep because you were making love the previous night? It is not just sleep loss that is of issue but the reasons for it. It is what you tell yourself about why you lost sleep that determines its ill effects.

Don't worry if you can't get to sleep during the first several minutes. Few people can get to sleep within 15 minutes. In fact, researchers in sleep labs usually regard the person who can get to sleep in less than 15 minutes as sleep deprived. In such cases, this shortened "sleep latency" time is the result of a rebound effect, making up for sleep lost the previous night.

Sleep maintenance insomnia problems can also be overestimated. Everyone wakes up in the middle of the night. But if it takes you more than 1 1/2 hours to get back to sleep, you probably have sleep maintenance insomnia.

The health risks of sleep loss are exaggerated. Nobody ever died directly from sleep loss. It is true, however, that sleep deprivation is one of the major causes of accidents.

Dr. William Dement of Stanford University examined the world record holder for sleep loss. After achieving the Guinness World Record for sleep loss, the individtual had no major adverse consequences.

The most severe effect of sleep loss is drowsiness. Moderate sleep loss has generally been shown to negatively affect mood, but mood is not affected in the same way by all people. If you find yourself becoming angry and concerned about sleep loss, then the negative effect on mood will be greater than if you just take it in stride. Those of us that are parents remember well the sleep loss associated with having a newborn in the house. But we were focused on the newborn, not the sleep loss. In contrast, insomniacs overreact and overestimate their sleep loss.

Some people resort to using over-the-counter sleep aids, commonly called "sleeping pills." If you use sleeping pills you probably found that they can initially contribute to sleep, but the quality of sleep is poor and you end up feeling less rested in the morning. Like alcohol, sleeping pills suppress important stages of sleep. They can also lead to tolerance and withdrawal. In other words, you will need more of the drug to achieve the same effect. Also, when you try to get to sleep without the sleep medication you will have a more difficult time sleeping than if you had never used that medication.

Most people who perform shift work also report having insomnia. Shift work results in the disruption of the melatonin circadian rhythm. Generally, the following problems have been correlated with shift work:

- Irritability.
- Sleepiness at work.

- Sleep disruption when sleeping—hearing noise, seeing light.
- Increase in work error and accidents.
- Carbohydrate craving.
- Weight gain.
- Susceptibility to stress.

Unfortunately, many companies still insist that their employees work rotating shifts. For people who have no choice but to adjust to their companies policy of shift work, there are a few concerns to keep in mind. It is advisable to try to maintain a consistent work schedule, but if you have to rotate, try to insist on a clockwise rotation. In other words, shift from evening to night to morning rather than night to evening to morning. People adjust better to staying up longer than forcing themselves to go to sleep earlier.

Try to eat frequent small meals and get regular exercise before work. When you get home go right to sleep. Often shift workers try to go to sleep in a lighted room. This is a mistake because the exposure to light delays your ability to sleep, because melatonin production will be low. If you are a shift worker, make sure that the room is completely dark. Also, try to get exposure to full spectrum light as soon as you wake up.

Factors That Induce Insomnia

There are a wide range of factors that have been found to contribute to insomnia, including aging, medical conditions, and drugs. For example, as we age the quality of our sleep deteriorates. We wake up more and spend more time in light sleep. To complicate this problem, many older people spend time indoors and are exposed to less light. Thus, their circadian rhythm is thrown off. Also, when people lose social cues, such as eating dinner at a set time or waking up at odd times, there is a stronger chance for their sleep cycle to become disrupted.

During menopause many women experience "hot flashes." Because the body temperature goes up during a hot flash, it is quite common that a woman will experience troubled sleep as a result.

Caffeine causes insomnia because it blocks adenosine, a sleep promoter, receptors in the brain. Because caffeine suppresses adenosine, it also suppresses sleep. Moreover, adenosine is responsible for promoting slow-wave sleep. Researchers at Stanford University report that because of this caffeine/adenosine antagonism, caffeine suppresses slow-wave sleep.

Many people try to improve their sleep by using techniques that actually exacerbate their sleep problem. For example, though you may feel sedated after drinking a "night cap," alcohol can by itself (with no job stress) create a sleep problem. As noted earlier, alcohol contributes to a reduction of the deepest stage of sleep (Stage 4) and REM sleep. Alcohol can also contribute to mid-sleep cycle awakening because the alcohol is wearing off during your sleep.

It has been estimated that 10 percent of all sleep maintenance problems are caused by alcohol. Therefore, you should not consume more than one drink per day and should insure that you consume the drink several hours before bedtime.

If you suffer from insomnia, don't use your computer in the late evening. Your insomnia will worsen. When you look at the computer screen for extended periods of time you are essentially looking at light. This light tricks your brain into adjusting to a daytime pattern. Light suppresses your pineal gland's ability to secrete melatonin, which is needed to be able to go to sleep. Your body clock can become maladapted to the actual day/night cycle. You need soft light a few hours before going to sleep.

There are also numerous medical conditions that have been associated with insomnia. It is important that you do not confuse the cause of your insomnia with a medical condition. Some of the medical causes of insomnia include:

- Fibromyalgia.
- Huntingtons's disease.
- Kidney disease.
- Hyperthyroidism.
- Parkinson's disease.
- Epilepsy.
- Cancer.
- Asthma.
- Hypertension.
- Heart disease.
- Bronchitis.
- Arthritis.

Unfortunately, there are several treatments for medical conditions that have been found to cause insomnia. Many physicians do not take the time to warn patients that insomnia is a side effect of the medication prescribed. The following list is just a sampling of the medications that contribute to insomnia:

- Decongestants.
- Corticosteroids.
- Diuretics.
- Heart medications.
- Parkinson's medications.
- Asthma medications.
- Appetite suppressants.
- Kidney medications.

Sleep Regimen

There are several ways you can improve your sleep, including exercise, diet, light exposure during the day, and keeping your bedroom cool at night.

Exercising three to six hours before bedtime helps you sleep better because you will be pushing your heart rate up and still allow enough time for it to drop before sleep. Even more importantly, by exercising you raise your body temperature and allow it to fall in time for bedtime. Aerobic exercise not only has a calming and antidepressant effect, but it also helps you.

If you can't manage to fit exercise into your busy schedule, consider it mandatory. Researchers at Stanford University studied the effect of exercise on sleep in adults 55 to 75 and found that those that exercised more than 20 to 30 minutes in the afternoon reduced the time that it took to go to sleep by one half.

The amount of light you are exposed to during the day also affects your sleep. If you maximize your bright light exposure during the daytime, you will set your body clock to match the natural day/ night cycle of the world around you. If you have early insomnia, expose yourself to bright light in the early morning. Not only will you insure that melatonin production will be low throughout the day but you will also insure that your body temperature will be the lowest when you sleep.

If you have sleep maintenance insomnia, expose yourself to bright light in the late morning. You will insure that your body temperature will be the lowest in the middle hours of your sleep cycle so that you will be able to stay asleep.

Keep your body temperature cool at night so that you can sleep deeply. Warm body temperatures promote light sleeps; therefore, keep your bedroom cool at night.

You may ask, "If staying cool is best, why do people say take a warm bath to relax before going to sleep?" Hot baths have been found to be helpful in winding down. Though you will be raising body temperature initially, your body temperature will drop sharply by bedtime.

Diet also has a major effect on sleep. If you eat foods rich in tryptophan you will become sleepy, because tryptophan is an amino acid that converts to serotonin. Simple carbohydrates such as white bread are not as helpful as complex carbohydrates such as wheat bread. Simple carbohydrates increase insulin, which in turn will increase tryptophan to serotonin. But this conversion will be on a short-term basis. Then your blood glucose will rise and you may wake up. On the other hand, if you eat complex carbohydrates you will trigger a serotonin conversion on a long-term basis and a slow and sustained rise in glucose.

Vitamins can also affect your sleep. Deficiencies in B-vitamins, calcium, and magnesium may inhibit sleep. Taking a calcium-magnesium tablet at night will promote relaxation and help with the restless leg syndrome.

Because your brain is geared to pay attention to novelty, you should insure that there are few sounds to grab your attention. Don't keep the television on at night; it will periodically grab your attention and wake you up. "White noise," on the other hand, is boring and monotonous and serves as a good screen for other noises, such as barking dogs. Some people keep a fan on all night long to provide white noise. Another useful technique is to use good quality earplugs to filter out noises.

Make sure that the time you spend in bed is only for sleep or sex. If you toss and turn more than 1 1/2 hours, get up and go to another room. By getting out of bed you will allow your body temperature to drop. If you lie there thinking about the fact that you are still awake you will charge up your brain wave and neurotransmitters associated with wakefulness.

Don't try too hard to go to sleep; the opposite will happen. Research has shown that trying to fall asleep promotes the release neurotransmitters, epinephrine and norepinephrine, which are activators and increase muscle tension, heart rate, blood pressure, and stress hormones. A vivid example of how this occurs was demonstrated in a contest. People were offered a cash prize to get to sleep quickest. The participants took twice as long as they usually do to fall asleep.

Many people do all the wrong things to try to sleep. Sonia was one of these people. After three months of job stress she found her sleep deteriorating. Each day she dragged herself into work wondering if she would be able to concentrate because of her terrible night of sleep. She tried to wake herself up with four cups of coffee, but just became more anxious as a result. By the time she left work she felt depressed and anxious.

Once at home she managed to make dinner for her family but did not have the appetite to eat herself. After watching them eat, she retired to bed complaining that she was too exhausted to stay up any longer. But in bed she found herself tossing and turning and thinking about work. She kept the television on despite the fact that she told everyone that she had no interest in television. After a week of suffering from miserable sleep she decided to drink a "night cap" to get a little sleep. Within 10 minutes after drinking a glass of wine she felt sedated. She managed to get to sleep for two hours, but then woke up with a jolt. She found it much more difficult to sleep than ever before.

Finally, Sonia decided to go to see her primary care physician to ask for sleep medication. Little did she know that he had just returned from a seminar on sleep. He declined to prescribe medication but did make several recommendations:

- Cut her caffeine intake.
- Force herself to eat three meals a day.
- Take a half-hour walk in the evening after coming home from work.
- Cut her alcohol entirely.
- Turn off the television in her bedroom.
- Eat a light snack with complex carbohydrates before going to sleep.

Though Sonia was disappointed that the doctor didn't prescribe medications, she agreed to go along with his recommendations. Within a few days of complaints about making these changes she began to have no trouble going to sleep or sleeping through the night. By the time she saw her physician two weeks later, her sleep had improved significantly.

Had her physician prescribed a sleeping aid and not made the recommendations she may have gotten a few nights of sleep. But she would have become dependent on the medication and needed more to sleep. As a result, she may have found herself more depressed.

Treating Insomnia

Millions of people treat their insomnia with either over-the-counter sleep drugs or physician prescribed benzodiazepines. The over-the-counter sleep aids such as Sominex and Excedrin PM have Benadryl within them and therefore produce some sedation. But it has been shown that these sleep aids have a significant placebo effect. In other words, they have been shown to have a similar effect to taking a pill that has no medicinal compound in it save the belief that it is a medicine. Belief itself is part of the medicine.

Recently, two major surveys of hundreds of studies on the effectiveness of treatment for insomnia have shown that sleep medications are relatively ineffective. Benzodiazepines are half as effective as behavioral approaches, and are simply not effective as a long-term treatment of insomnia. If you take them on a regular basis, you will have daytime grogginess, shallow sleep, and suffer from withdrawals when you try sleeping without them, making it even harder to sleep.

Therefore, you should only consider benzodiazepines as a short-term treatment for acute insomnia. If you are looking for a solution beyond a few nights sleep don't take benzodiazepines. In fact, one of the key goals of the Harvard University Insomnia Program is the withdrawal off all sleep medications.

If you are taking sleep medication, don't abruptly withdraw from them. Your withdrawal should be a gradual tapering process that is self-paced. At the Kaiser Permanente Medical Centers we recommend that withdrawal from benzodiazepines be done under physician supervision. The following guidelines are important:

1. Reduce your dose on one night a week. For the first night it is advisable to choose an easy night, such as a weekend night.

2. On the second week, reduce your dose on two nights a week. But space the nights apart to insure that they are not consecutive nights.

3. Continue this pattern until you are down to your lowest possible dose for all nights.

4. Follow the same procedure with no medication at night.

For a long-term solution to insomnia, use a cognitive-behavioral approach. This approach includes a change in your bedtime schedule and how you think about sleep.

Sleep scheduling involves instituting changes in the time you go to sleep. By adjusting the time you go to bed, you will be building up "sleep pressure" to go to sleep and stay asleep through the night. This is based on the fact that people who are sleep deprived fall asleep earlier the next night to "catch up" on lost sleep.

If you have chronic insomnia, your sleep cycle is not that easily corrected. Hopefully, you aren't like many people who suffer from chronic insomnia and try to adjust to the sleep deprivation by doing precisely the wrong things to "catch up." They try to sleep longer in the morning only to make it more difficult to sleep the next night.

The sleep scheduling approach requires that you get up in the morning at the same time each morning despite how much sleep you managed the previous night. But, instead of going to bed earlier you will be going to bed later. You may think, "If I'm sleep deprived, I need to allow myself as much chance to sleep as possible, even if I toss and turn."

Calculate how many hours you actually do sleep on average and add one more hour. Use this formula to schedule how much sleep time you will allow yourself. For example, if you were averaging 5 1/2 hours of sleep for the past month despite staying in bed 8 1/2 hours, allow yourself 6 1/2 hours of potential sleep time. If your normal wake-up time has been 6 a.m. go to bed at 11:30 p.m. Do this for at least four weeks. Your goal will be to fill up most of that bedtime with sleep. Eventually your body temperature will adjust and the sleep pressure will build up so that you can make another adjustment to add another hour to be able to sleep for 7 1/2 hours.

This approach is useful for people who have chronic insomnia, not for people who have experienced a night or two of poor sleep. For chronic insomniacs, the task at hand is to repair your sleep cycle. Your sleep cycle is out of synch and sleep scheduling helps it get back into synch. By practicing sleep scheduling you will be increasing sleep efficiency.

Sleep researchers have found that most people have embraced several myths about sleep. Therefore, part of the Harvard Sleep Program centers on how we have developed myths about sleep and how the perpetuation of these myths feed insomnia.

Here is how chronic insomnia develops: Usually insomnia begins because of a stressful event such as job stress. Perhaps you felt harassed by your supervisor and experienced a few nights of trouble sleeping. But then the insomnia problem is prolonged if you worry about not being able to sleep. The following chain of thoughts and events can lead to a "learned" insomnia problem:

When going to sleep you may say to yourself, "I'm not going to get to sleep tonight."

Sleep is more difficult to attain.

The bed becomes an enemy—a negative cue.

You may try to sleep later on the weekends to compensate.

While back in bed the next night you begin to feel as though you are losing sleep.

You try too hard to get to sleep.

The thoughts about sleep add to daytime stress.

Negative sleep thoughts (NSTs) push temporary insomnia into long-term insomnia. NSTs are essentially inaccurate ideas about sleep that create a self-fulfilling prophecy. Here are some common NSTs:

- I have to get the same number of hours of sleep every night.
- There is something wrong with me.

- I will never get to sleep.
- I will be ruined tomorrow.
- I can't get my mind to turn off.

If you believe these NSTs, then you will have more difficulty falling asleep again because of the build up of stress. Dr. Gregory Jacobs, director of Harvard's sleep program, stresses the importance of challenging these NSTs because they push temporary insomnia into long-term insomnia.

NSTs will result in negative feelings such as anger and all of the biochemical changes associated with it, all of which are activating, not sedating. NSTs set off a chain of events that result in insomnia. The chain looks something like this:

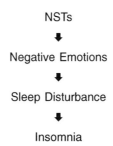

NSTs
↓
Negative Emotions
↓
Sleep Disturbance
↓
Insomnia

Jacobs asks patients to identify their false thoughts and replace them with accurate information about sleep. For example, if you wake up in the middle of the night, you may interpret your wakefulness in one of the following ways:

- This isn't great but at least I've got my core sleep.
- If I don't get a good night's sleep tonight I will tomorrow night.
- I may get back to sleep, I may not. Either way it is not the end of the world.

The irony is that adopting these thoughts will better enable you to get back to sleep if you wake up. This is based on the fact that trying too hard to sleep contributes to stress, which prevents sleep. By adopting the accurate thoughts about sleep you will take the pressure off yourself and probably relax enough to get to sleep. In addition, while you are lying in bed awake, you might as well use the time to relax. Relaxation methods are helpful to quiet the mind down.

Practicing relaxation during daytime will help you sleep at night. Relaxation methods work best if practiced twice daily, once during the day and once before bed. They serve to reduce the effect of stress. Relaxation audiotapes have been shown to be helpful. However, some people complain that they are annoyed when the tape recorder clicks off. Try to make sure that your tape player can turn itself off without a click or click it off yourself so that you remain in control of the process.

Angela managed to learn many of these techniques after a period of chronic insomnia. Initially she had a very difficult time falling asleep at night when she began to endure constant harassment by her unit supervisor. As a seamstress she had been working as quickly she as possibly could. But management made it clear that production needed to improve or the company was in trouble. When the company was sold, new management required an even faster pace. To make matters worse her supervisor was constantly criticizing her in front of her peers.

Night after night Angela tossed and turned thinking such thoughts as, "I'm never going to get any sleep," and "There is something wrong with me." Every morning she found herself feeling fatigued and irritable. Finally she decided to do something about her insomnia. Her sister talked her into going for a consultation at the sleep center at the local university. At Angela's first appointment she complained that "I'm so tired at work that I can't even concentrate on the TV in the bedroom, but I still can't sleep. Then I try to make up the lost sleep on the weekends."

She was disturbed to hear the psychologist, Dr. Somni, tell her not to try to make up the sleep on the weekends and to move the television set out of her room. She found it particularly disturbing that he asked her to wake up the same time on the weekends and to go to bed one hour later each night. She said to her sister, "He's crazy. I'm not going back there!"

Her sister countered by telling her that she recently read in the local newspaper that since its inception the center had helped hundreds of insomniacs. After her sister asked, "What do you have to lose?" Angela agreed to return. She went along with Dr. Somni's recommendations "just to prove to him that they don't work."

By the time she returned for her next visit her sleep was improving. Dr. Somni told her that if she woke up in the middle of the night to tell herself not to be alarmed because she had been getting her core sleep anyway. He also told her that building up sleep pressure would allow her to go to bed one hour earlier.

After one week, Angela reported that she was able to get one more hour of sleep. She continued to follow the plan and within two weeks she found that she had returned to a normal sleep cycle, despite the job stress.

If you have chronic insomnia like Angela, you don't need to wait to go to a sleep program to get started with a change to your sleep pattern. Following is a list of techniques that have contributed to better sleep:

1. Do not do anything in your bed other than sleep (except for sex). Do not watch television, balance your checkbook, discuss finances with your spouse, or argue in bed. Make your bed carry only one association—sleep.
2. If you cannot sleep and find yourself tossing and turning, get up and go to another room.
3. Do not "try too hard" to go to sleep. You will frustrate yourself, which will lead to a paradoxical effect. Tell yourself, "It's okay if I get just a few hours sleep tonight. I will catch up the next night." This change in expectation will free you up to be able to relax and get to sleep. The harder you try to go to sleep the harder it will be to induce sleep.
4. Avoid drinking large quantities of liquid at night. This will lower the sleep threshold and cause you to wake up to urinate.
5. Avoid bright light at least a few hours before going to sleep. Don't work on the computer into the late evening.
6. Do all planning for the next day before you get into bed. If you think of something you need to remember, get up and write it down. Tell yourself that you will postpone thinking or worrying about anything until the next day.
7. Avoid all daytime naps. Think of naps as a way to steal sleep from the nighttime.
8. Try eating a light snack with complex carbohydrates before bed. Foods rich with L-tryptophan are advisable. Don't eat anything with sugar or salt before bed.

9. Avoid protein snacks at night because protein blocks the synthesis of serotonin and as a result promotes alertness.

10. Exercise three to six hours before you go to bed.

11. If noise bothers you, use earplugs.

12. Avoid alcohol.

13. If you are troubled by chronic insomnia try the sleep scheduling technique.

14. Try the relaxation exercises described in Chapter 18. These will help you go to sleep or go back to sleep if you wake up during the night.

CHAPTER 18

Relax

YOU MAY THINK THAT LEARNING to relax is next to impossible during a period of job stress. But it's true that learning relaxation techniques can neutralize the tension you feel from job stress. You will learn many of these techniques in this chapter.

Just as Harvard Professor Walter Cannon had drawn attention to the fight-or-flight response, another Harvard professor, Herbert Benson, drew attention to what he dubbed the "relaxation response." This is your body's way of calming itself down. The relaxation response involves lowering the heart rate, metabolism, and slowing down breathing.

Fight or Flight Response	Relaxation Response
↑ Heart rate	↓ Heart rate
↑ Blood pressure	↓ Blood pressure
↑ Metabolism	↓ Metabolism
↑ Muscle tension	↓ Muscle tension
↑ Breathing rate	↓ Breathing rate
↑ Mental arousal	↓ Mental arousal

Table 18.1 The body's response to stress and relaxation

In Chapter 1, you learned that you have a sympathetic nervous system and a parasympathetic nervous system. While the sympathetic nervous system activates our body during the fight-or-flight response, the parasympathetic nervous system calms you down as during the relaxation response. In this chapter, I will describe how you can activate your parasympathetic nervous system and promote the relaxation response.

You can induce the relaxation response by a variety of techniques. Most relaxation techniques involve "letting go" of sympathetic arousal by shifting your attention away from the anxiety-provoking aspects of your situation. Because trying "too hard" to relax will actually make you more stressed, letting go allows your body (through the parasympathetic nervous system) to calm down. Letting go can be counterintuitive. If you try to relax you will probably stay tense.

Letting go is a passive process. By *allowing* yourself to relax instead of *trying* to relax, you take the pressure off yourself. For example, try not to think of pink elephants. By forcing yourself to keep pink elephants out of your mind, you fight with yourself and invariably think of pink elephants. Now focus on something else such as blue kangaroos. Tell yourself that if pink elephants pop into your mind, so be it. You probably won't think about pink elephants now because your attention has shifted and you let go of the pressure that you put on yourself to keep pink elephants out of your mind. Similarly, if you try not to be tense you will probably make yourself more tense. But by focusing on relaxation the tension can melt away because you have shifted your attention to relaxation.

There are a number of techniques that you can employ to achieve relaxation, but all involve shifting attention and letting go. Some of these techniques are generally referred to as relaxation techniques, while others fall under the broad categories of self-hypnosis, autogenic training, visual imagery, and meditation. All of these techniques involve a focus on breathing.

Breathing

You may take the importance of breathing for granted and not know that different breathing patterns promote different emotional states. Your breathing rate naturally speeds up when you are experiencing stress. Muscles in the abdomen tighten up and your chest cavity is constricted.

Because you have a cardiovascular system, a system in which your respiratory system and circulatory system are connected, rapid breathing will make your heart rate speed up and make you more anxious. On the other hand, if you slow down your breathing and heart rate, you will probably become more relaxed.

Most people breathe from nine to 16 breaths per minute when they are at rest. Panic attacks often involve as much 27 breaths per minute. With accelerating breathing alone, anyone can experience many of the symptoms we associate with a panic attack including numbness, tingling, dry mouth, and light-headedness.

Breathing too fast is referred to as hyperventilation or "overbreathing." If you overbreathe you will pull in too much oxygen, forcing down the carbon dioxide level in your blood stream. Carbon dioxide helps maintain the critical acid-base level in your blood. By lowering this level, your nerve cells become more excitable and make it more likely that you will feel anxiety or have a panic attack.

If you feel anxious, stop and watch your breath and then slow it down. Breathing deeply will help you to relax by shifting from the fight-or-flight response to the relaxation response, from the sympathetic to the parasympathetic nervous system.

Slow down your breathing rate by breathing "abdominally." As you breath abdominally, your belly rises with your inhale and drops with a exhale. This is because as you breathe abdominally, the large dome-shaped muscle that divides your thoracic cavity from the abdominal cavity below expands and contracts. When you exhale your diaphragm moves upward and your abdominal muscles contract, helping get rid of stale air or carbon dioxide. When you inhale, the diaphragm contracts, pulling it down and the abdominal muscles relax. This allows for the expansion of your lower lungs.

Thus, abdominal/diaphragmatic breathing allows you to get more oxygen in and more carbon dioxide out. Because the entire process of breathing is to oxygenate your blood and expel waste air (carbon dioxide), diaphragmatic breathing allows you to get more fuel (oxygen) to each organ.

Try abdominal breathing next time you feel anxious. Notice how the anxiety drifts away.

Hatha Yoga

Hatha yoga is a method of stretching and relaxation that can help you deal with stress. The practice of Hatha yoga takes a series of postures, some of which involve stretching, and combines them with meditation and deep breathing. It has been shown after 40 years of research that accomplished yogis are able to calm themselves and have control

over a variety of body functions. For example, many yogis have demonstrated that they can slow their heart rate down to that achieved in
deep sleep, though they are not sleeping.

The Progressive Relaxation Method

One of the most popular relaxation techniques is referred to
as Progressive Relaxation. It involves tensing and releasing your
muscles. Your task is to tense and release a particular muscle group,
such as your fingers or toes, while simultaneously breathing deeply.

Start with your feet by spreading your toes and keeping your
muscles in your feet tense while you count to 10. Then release the
muscles and notice and enjoy the flow of relaxation for at least 20
seconds. Tense and relax three times.

Now splay your fingers for 10 seconds. Release your muscles
and notice the relaxing feelings. Move to your calf muscles, then
forearms, thighs, upper arms, upper legs, pelvic area, stomach
muscles, chest muscles, shoulders, neck, and your entire face and
scalp.

Try to remember not to tense too hard, but just enough to feel the
tension. Make this a meditative exercise. Do not rush through the
exercise; it is not aerobic.

Now that you have completed the exercise, breathe easily and
watch very closely how the muscles in your body are limp and relaxed.
Imagine them being heavy while you notice that your mind is light
and airy.

The relaxation period at the end of the exercise will carry into the
next hour whatever you may be engaged in, going to work or simply
unwinding after work. But the progressive relaxation method is not
effective to use to combat insomnia, because the tense portion of the
technique does not dissipate enough for sleep. However, it is a useful
technique in dissipating daytime stress.

Imagery

Imagery is a relaxation technique that has gained popularity over
the past 20 years. It's practice involves visualizing being in a tranquil
place that gives you a sense of peace. For example, imagine yourself
in a mountain meadow with the sun shining on your back or at the

beach watching the waves roll in, one after the other. Imagine the vivid details of a mountain meadow or beach. Concentrate on all of the visual and tactile sensations.

Concentrate on the sound of the surf ebbing and flowing, just like your breath. Concentrate on the bird sitting on a tree branch. The bird looks at you, then gracefully flies away. Feel the sun on your back gently warming you.

Imagery takes you away on a break from all of the stress of the day. If you fully absorb yourself in the scenes that you imagine you will return to work refreshed and vitalized.

Self-Hypnosis

Hypnosis is a form of relaxation that utilizes both breathing and imagery. It is much easier to do than you might assume, but first you have to dispel the myths that have developed about hypnosis:

- Patients are under the hypnotist's control.
- The same techniques are used for all people.
- A person in hypnotic trance will be unconscious.
- You can't get out of the trance without a special ritual.
- Only a small group of patients are susceptible to hypnosis.

Hypnosis, similar to meditation and relaxation training, is a form of concentration, focused attention, and increased receptivity to suggestion and direction. Hypnosis is a method of focused relaxation.

Self-hypnosis is essentially the same thing as hypnosis only without the hypnotist as an aid. The type of self-hypnosis that I teach people involves focused breath and counting from 10 to 1. While decreasing in numbers, you can imagine particular parts of your body relaxing on every exhale.

It is particularly important, while going through this exercise, to remind yourself that you can "step out of the way" so that your body can relax itself. This point is important because it is so often the case that we keep ourselves tense throughout the day. If you "allow" your body a chance to do what is natural for it, the process of relaxation can happen.

Try the following steps and use any of the following phrases:

10: I am allowing the tension to leave my body with every exhale.

9: I am feeling my body become heavy.

8: Sounds, physical sensations, and thoughts are occurring around my external self, all way up on the surface. I am deep within myself.

7: I feel like I am descending deeper within myself, as if I am going down an escalator.

6: I don't need to fight the relaxation. I can visualize myself drifting with the current down the river. I don't need to swim up stream.

5: I am falling deep within myself and gently swaying like a feather that slowly sways back and forth as it falls to the ground.

4: I am deep within myself without worry and time.

3: I am letting go of the external world.

2: Relaxation and I are one.

1: I am at peace with myself.

Hypnosis has been found to have numerous positive effects. By developing the ability to do self-hypnosis, you will be in a far better position to shed stress and take a calming command of your life. The following are often cited as effects of self-hypnosis:

- Reduced anxiety and fear.
- Decreased requirements for analgesics.
- Increased comfort level during medical procedures.
- Greater stability of functions of autonomic nervous system (such as decreased blood pressure).
- Enhanced sense of self-control.

Autogenic Training

Autogenic Training is a relaxation technique developed by Oscar Vogt and Johannes Shultz. It employs the concept of "passive concentration" on particular areas of your body. The practitioners of autogenic training repeat phrases to themselves, such as "I feel quiet...my neck, my jaw, and forehead feel relaxed." You can use warmth phrases such as "My hands, my arm feel warm and heavy."

You can use reverie phrases such as "My thoughts are turned inward and I am at ease. Deep within my mind I feel at peace and calm quietness." And you can use activation phrases such as "I feel life and energy flowing through my chest, arms, and hands."

If you practice autogenic training, you will notice some similarities between it and progressive relaxation. However, unlike progressive relaxation the focus is primarily on relaxation; no tension is required.

Graded Steps:

- Comfortable posture.
- Feeling heavy in limbs.
- Warmth in legs and arms.
- Autonomy of breathing ("it breathes me").
- Feelings of peacefulness.
- Calm heart beat.
- Warmth in upper abdomen.
- Coolness of forehead.

By using relaxing phrases you can take yourself progressively through these graded steps for different parts of your body. For example:

- My feet feel warm and heavy…
- My ankles feel warm and relaxed…
- My hips feel relaxed and heavy…
- My abdomen feels warm and relaxed…
- My chest feels relaxed…
- My neck feels comfortable and relaxed…
- My arms feel heavy and warm…
- My arms feels warm and relaxed
- My forehead feels smooth and relaxed…
- My jaw feels relaxed and comfortable…
- My whole body feels heavy, relaxed, and comfortable…

Body Scan

The body scan technique can be a variant of mindfulness meditation. It is also very similar to Autogenic Training. Your task is to scan your body and with every exhale focus on a particular body area. For example, start with your feet and feel the weight of your feet, the blood flowing through them, and the muscles being softened by the weight and blood flow. Whatever feeling you have in your feet, tension or lack of tension, just feel it. Do not fight or try too hard to relax. Just observe. Now move to your calves and do the same thing. Then move to your knees, thighs, and so on up your body, just observing and letting go.

The Sigh of Relief

A quick and easy way to let go of tension is to breathe in deeply, then exhale a deep sigh, "Ahhh…." By letting go of tension with a sigh you will allow yourself a quick fix of relief. The sigh of relief is a release or a shedding of tension that can be practiced though the day several times.

Biofeedback

Biofeedback is technique that uses electrical instruments to provide information about how you are using your body. The point of using these instruments is to allow you a clear means to learn how to relax. The term "biofeedback" means that the "bio" (your body) gets "feedback" (visual or auditory signals) regarding the tension or relaxation of the specific parts of your body.

Biofeedback is based on the concept that relaxation can be achieved by "visceral learning" or "operant conditioning." This concept applied to biofeedback means that by paying close attention to how relaxed or warm a particular part of your body is, you can "shape" your behavior to achieve a complete sense of relaxation. For example, one instrument, referred to as the Galvanic Skin Response (GSR), will give you information on how warm your hand is by showing a gauge that records temperature. By watching the gauge closely you can concentrate on increasing the blood flow to your hand and thereby warming it up.

The following biofeedback instruments are those commonly used to promote relaxation.

Electromyographic (EMG) Biofeedback

Measures:

Muscle Tension

Method:

Sensors attached to skin detect electrical activity (i.e., muscle tension in a specific area is monitored). For example, electrode sensors are taped on your forehead to measure the frontalis muscle, so often tensed up to produce a tension headache. Your task is to learn to relax the frontalis muscle.

Treatment of:

- Tension headaches.
- Chronic muscle pain.
- Incontinence.
- General relaxation.

Thermal Biofeedback

Measures:

Temperature of skin, as an index of blood flow changes in dilation or constriction of blood vessels.

Method:

Temperature sensitive probe ("thermistor") is taped to skin, often the finger.

Treatment of:

- Raynaud's disease.
- Migraine headaches.
- Hypertension.
- Anxiety.

Electrodermal Activity (EDA)

Measures:

Changes in sweat activity too small to feel.

Method:

Two sensors are attached to the palm side of fingers producing a tiny electrical current measuring skin conductance based on the amount of moisture present.

Treatment of:

- Anxiety.
- Hyperhidrosis (overactive sweat glands).

Finger Pulse

Measures:

Pulse rate and force (amount of blood in each pulse).

Method:

A sensor is attached to a finger. Helps measure heart activity as a sign of arousal of part of autonomic nervous system.

Treatment of:

- Hypertension.
- Anxiety.
- Some cardiac arrhythmia.

Breathing

Measures:

Breath rate, volume, rhythm and location (chest and abdomen).

Method:

Sensors attached to chest and abdomen.
Also measures airflow from mouth and nose.
Goal: regular breaths using abdominal muscles.

Treatment of:

- Asthma.
- Hyperventilation.
- Anxiety.

Electroencephalograph

Measures:

Brain waves.

Method:

Sensors are attached to the head, and the person or his aid gives feedback on whether or not a relaxed set of brain waves is achieved.

Treatment of:

- Tension.

Induces:

- Alpha and periodic theta waves.
- Synchronized brain waves for both hemispheres.
- Changes in GSR.
- Decreased respiration rate.
- Decreased oxygen consumption.

• • •

Overall biofeedback has been shown to be quite helpful in aiding people in the following areas:

- Physical self-regulation.
- Increased blood pressure.
- Teeth clenching and grinding.
- Incontinence.
- Muscle disorders.
- Tension headaches.
- Anxiety.
- Chronic pain.

Biofeedback instruments have been used to research various types of relaxation techniques. For example, meditation has been widely researched. It has consistently been found that meditation has produced several positive biophysiological effects as measured by biofeedback instruments.

Meditation and Prayer

Most religions have literature, including manuals, on meditation and prayer. Within Hinduism, Buddhism, Sufism, Judaism, and Christianity, meditation and prayer have had a long tradition and have been practiced for thousands of years. It was not until late in the 20th century that the effects of meditation and prayer were thoroughly researched. In the United States, meditation grew in popularity in the late 1960s, first with Transcendental Meditation, often referred to as "TM."

Much of the early research on meditation was based on the practice of TM. From the beginning, it was found that TM promoted calming effects. Later research has shown that most types of meditation and prayer help people relax themselves.

Most types of meditation involve clearing your mind and focusing on your breathing. You can clear your mind by concentrating on a few words—referred to them as a mantra, such as Sat Nam. By concentrating on the mantra, your tendency to think about your job will drift away. Concentrating on your breath can also help clear your mind and help you relax.

After trying with some success to deal with her job stress by diet, exercise, and seeing a counselor, Margaret still felt tense. She felt that she changed what she could at work but still found her thoughts racing from one worry to another. She worried that she was just a tense person. Then, when her friend Nancy invited her to her weekly meditation sitting and lecture, Margaret said, "Oh, I might as well."

During the lecture and meditation exercise, Margaret's thoughts were everywhere but in the present. On the way home she said, "I don't exactly get it. All your people were just sitting there with your eyes closed. What was the point of all that?"

Nancy smiled, "We were all just quieting our minds."

"But what's the point of sitting there with a bunch of people? I just started thinking about who they were and why they came."

"Well, getting together with others just adds support and encouragement to keep on practicing. Also we come for the talk. What did you think?"

"I'm not sure if I know what he meant by breathing your mantra."

"The point he was trying to make was that you must concentrate on a mantra—you know the word you use on your inhale and the one you use on exhale. If you do that, it will help slow things down. Don't you want to slow things down a bit?"

"Well, yeah. It's seems that my mind has been racing a thousand miles an hour for the last few months...should I quit?....find another job—all that!"

"You need to learn to take a break from all that mental turmoil. That's where this meditation comes in. It will help you take a break from all that."

Despite the fact that she didn't believe Nancy, Margaret tried it the next session. She found herself feeling more relaxed. She practiced at home, and soon she found herself looking forward to her next session.

Technique	Oxygen Consumption	Respiratory Rate	Heart Rate	Alpha Waves	Blood Pressure	Muscle Tension
TM Meditation	Decreases	Decreases	Decreases	Increases	Decreases*	(Not measured)
Zen and Yoga	Decreases	Decreases	Decreases	Increases	Decreases*	(Not measured)
Autogenic Training	(Not measured)	Decreases	Decreases	Increases	(Results inconclusive)	Decreases
Progressive Relaxation	(Not measured)	(Not measured)	(Not measured)	(Not measured)	(Results inconclusive)	Decreases
Hypnosis With Suggested Deep Relaxation	Decreases	Decreases	Decreases	(Not measured)	(Results inconclusive)	(Not measured)

*In patients with elevated blood pressure

Table 18.1. Meditation effects

Gradually, the effects of her now daily meditation exercises spread subtly through the day. She became less anxious and better able to deal with the stress at work.

Whatever type of relaxation technique you practice, regard it as important as eating or sleeping. Begin to structure relaxation into part of your day and workweek. Ritualize the process of relaxation by picking a particular time, say 10 to 40 minutes before or after a shower. Making relaxation a ritual anoints it as important as sitting down for dinner.

You may say to yourself, "I don't have time to do all this!" Not all relaxation exercises need be lengthy in time. You can take just a few moments to slow down your breathing and drop your shoulders. You can remind yourself throughout the day to take a few moments to relax by placing a blue dot on the steering wheel or your wristwatch. When you see the dot you can stop for perhaps five seconds to collect yourself and breathe deeply. You can even identify certain objects as a cue to relax. A doorknob or a desk drawer can serve as a reminder to take just a few moments and relax. However you practice relaxation, it can be an important antidote to job stress.

APPENDIX

Recommended Readings and Internet Resources

Recommended Reading

Benson, Herbert and Eileen Stuart. *The Wellness Book.* New York: Fireside, 1992.

Benson, Herbert. *The Mind/Body Effect.* New York: Simon & Schuster, 1979.

Borysenko, Joan. *Mending the Body, Mending the Mind.* Reading MA: Addison-Wesley, 1987.

Bourne, Edmund. *Anxiety and Phobia Workbook*. Oakland: New Harbinger Press, 2000.

Burns, David. *Feeling Good: The Feeling Good Handbook*. New York: Plume, 1999.

Cannon, Walter. *The Wisdom of the Body*. New York: W.W. Norton, 1935.

Kabot-Zin, Jon. *Full Catastrophe Living: Using the Wisdom of Your Body and Mind to Face Stress, Pain, and Illnesses*. New York: Delcort Press, 1990.

Friedman, Mayer and Ray Roseman. *Type A Behavior and Your Heart.* New York: Alfred Knopf, 1971.

Humphrey, James. *Job Stress*. Boston: Allyn and Bacon, 1995.

Lewinsohn, Peter M. (Editor) Rebecca Forster, and Mary A. Youngsen. *Control Your Depression*. New York: Simon & Schuster, 1992.

McKay, Mathew, Peter Rogers, and Judith McKay. *When Anger Hurts: Quieting the Storm Within*. Oakland, CA: New Harbinger Press, 1989.

Selye, Hans. *The Stress of Life*. New York: McGraw Hill, 1978.

—. *Stress Without Distress*. New York: New American Library, 1975.

Internet Resources

www.jobstresshelp.com

Job Stress Help, a page with links and facts.

www.health.org

Substance Abuse and Mental Health Services Administration Department of Health and Human Services (SAMHSA) National Clearinghouse for Alcohol and Drug Information.

www.mentalhealth.com/p1.html

Free encyclopedia of mental health information.

www.familiesandwork.org

A workplace resource.

www.plainsense.com/health/Stress/newjob.htm

A page with information regarding stress of a new job produced by the Plainsense pages (health resources).

www.cdc.gov/niosh/violpurp.html

Workplace violence produced by the National Institute of Occupational Safety and Health.

infoventures.com/osh

OSH-Link's Online Occupational Safety and Health Database (OSH-DB) is a bibliographic database covering virtually all aspects of the occupational safety and health field.

www.isma.org.uk

International Stress Management Association, United Kingdom. This British Web site offers information on stress management. It provides links to articles on stress, news regarding stress, and other Web sites.

www.osga.gov/oshinfo/priorities/violence.html

Occupational Safety and Health Administration (OSHA), US Department of Labor. This is the OSHA page that provides information on workplace violence. It also makes recommendations for workplace safety.

www.osha.gov

OSHA homepage. This is the main Occupational Safety and Health Administration Web site. It provides information on a wide variety of issues related to workplace safety.

www.dol.gov

This is the US Department of Labor Web site. It provides information on workers' compensation, wages, labor laws, and very much more.

www.eeoc.gov

This is the Web site for the US Equal Employment Opportunity Commission (EEOC). It provides information on discrimination, news, statistics, and how to contact EEOC.

www.unl.edu/stress/mgmt

This Web site is titled *Stress Management: A Review of Principles*. It is operated by Dr. Wesley Sime, Professor of Health and Human Performance at the University of Nebraska in Lincoln. He has provided information on stress, personality, relaxation, and much more.

www.stress.org

This Web site, *The American Institute of Stress*, is based in New York City. It provides information about stress, offers a newsletter, has a page on job stress, and gives reports on upcoming meetings. Other contact information is as follows: The American Institute of Stress, 124 Park Ave., Yonkers, NY 10703; Phone (914) 963-1200; Fax (914) 965-6267; e-mail: *stress124@earthlink.net*.

www.cdc.gov/niosh/stresswk.html

The National Institute for Occupational Safety and Health (NIOSH) is the Federal agency responsible for conducting research and making recommendations for the prevention of work-related illness and injury. NIOSH is part of the U.S. Department of Health and Human Services; it is distinct from the Occupational Safety and Health Administration (OSHA), which is a regulatory agency located in the U.S. Department of Labor.

INDEX

A

Action, 42, 44,

Adaptive, 21, 22

Aerobic boost, activities, 122

Affective constriction, 64

Alcohol, 62-67
  characteristics of drinkers, 65
  consequences, 63-67
  deficits in thinking ability,
    64-65
  facts, 62
  myths, 62

*American Psychological
  Association Monitor*, 20, 24

Amino acids, foods rich in, 50

Anandamide, 68

Anger
  examine the cause of your, 95
  management, 100
  neutralizing, 93

Antidepressants, 110

Anxiety, 27
  causes of, 34
  defusing the, 31
  symptoms and sensations,
    27-28

Ativan, 109, 110

Attitude adjustment,
  making an, 171

Autocratic style, 143

Autogenic training, 202-203

B

Bad thinking traps, 32

Balance your sanity, 140

Benzodiazepines, 109

Biofeedback, 204
  areas helpful in, 207

Black hole, avoiding the, 149

Blaming, 97

Body scan, 203

Body temperature cycle, 180

Boost,
  getting a, 53
  sugar, 54

Breathing, 198, 206

Bullies, 76

Burnout,
  consider it if, 105-106
  job, 105
  main symptoms, 105
  ways to avoid, 106

B-vitamins, 187

C

Caffeine, 55-59
 content, 56
 problems, 55
Catastrophizing, 40
Causes of anxiety,
 chemical and compound, 35
 medical, 35
 medications, 36
Causes of depression,
 drugs, 46
 foods, 52
 medical, 46
Chain of events,
 avoid setting off, 98-99
Chest expanding, 118
Classical conditioning, 31
Cognitive constriction, 64
Communicating, impersonal,
 avoiding, 131
Commute, adjustments to your,
 103-104
Computer-automated
 workplace, 129
Constructive thoughts, 30
Control
 losing, 92
 obsession, 32
Crash, getting a, 53
Crude labeling, 97

D

Depression, 37, 40, 41
 causes of, 45
 overcoming, 39

Depression, *(cont.)*
 symptoms of, 37-38
 thinking errors, 40
Direct put-downs, 98
Disability, 153
Dopamine, 63
Drug Free Workplace Act, 61

E

EAP, 159
EDA, 205-206
EEOC, 155, 156
Elavil, 110, 112
Electrodermal Activity, 205-206
Electroencephalograph, 206
Electromyographic
 Biofeedback, 204-205
Electronic performance
 monitoring system, 133
Emotional reasoning, 40
Employee assistance
 professional, 159
EPM, 133
Exaggeration, 96-97
Exercising, 120
 reasons for not, 120

F

FDA, 113
Fight-or-flight, 17-21, 197
 bodily changes during, 17
Finger pulse, 206
Fist clenching, 120

Food and Drug Administration, 113

Frustration, chain of events, 94

G

GABA, 62, 63, 68, 109, 115

GAD, 28
symptoms, 29

Galvanic Skin Response, 204

GCs, 64

Generalized Anxiety disorder, 28

Globalizing, 97

Glucocorticoids, 64

Gossip, 79, 89

Graded steps, 203

GSR, 204

H

Harassment, 11, 71
pertinent questions, 72
sexual, 71-76
two most common, 71
two types, 72

Hatha Yoga, 199

Health Maintenance Organization, 16

Herbs, 109, 113

High blood pressure, 54-55

HMO, 16

Hyperventilation, 199

Hypnosis, myths about, 201

I

Imagery, 200

I message, 101, 102

Impersonal communication, avoiding, 131-132

Insomnia, 18
factors that induce, 184
learned, chain of thoughts, 191
medical causes, 185
medications that contribute to, 186
treating, 189-190

International Survey Research Corporation, 15

Interview, 165
don'ts, 167
preparing tips, 166

Job fishing, 163
resume tips, 165
sources to check, 164

Job stress cost of, 15

Job transition, steps, 160-161

K

Kaiser Permanente Medical Center, 73

Kava Kava, 114-115

L

Laissez-faire supervisor, 143-144

LDL cholesterol, 55

Librium, 109

M

Maladaptive, 21, 22

MAO inhibitors, 110, 111

Marijuana, 67-69
   consequences and side
      effects, 67-68

Medical marijuana, 67

Medicine and herbs, 109

Medicines, 109

Meditation, 207
   effects, 209

Mind reading, 40, 97

Mistakes, to avoid making, 127

Monoamine inhibitors, 110

Mood state, 32

Moving on, questions to
   consider, 158-159

Moving, 120

N

Nanosecond, 137

National Institute for
   Occupational Safety and
      Health, 14

Neck roll, 119

Negative sleep thoughts,
   191-192

Net, the big, 163

Neurotransmitters, functions of,
   50

Neutral stimulus, 31

Next opportunity, points to keep
   in mind, 101

Nicotine, 55

NIOSH, 14, 15, 213

NLRB, 156

Norepinephrine, 57, 64

NST, 191-192
   chain of events, 192

O

OSHA, 213

OSSA, 156

Overgeneralization, 40

P

Panic spiral, 29
   chain or events, 29

Passivity, 82

Perfectionism, 32

Personalization, 40

Phobia, 28

Polarized thinking, 40

Polyunsaturated fats, foods high
   in, 52

Post-Traumatic Stress
   Syndrome, 24

Prayer, 207

Prayer/Hand Push, 119

Profanity, 98

Progressive relaxation method,
   200

Prozac, 112, 115

Pseudotelepathy, 97

Psychological complaints, 22-23

R

Random drug tests, 61
Rapid Eye Movement, 57, 63
Rational Phytotherapy, 114
Realistic thoughts, 41
Relaxation, 197
  steps and phrases to try, 202
Relaxing, 197
  phrases, 203
REM, 57, 62, 63, 178, 179
Respect , how to earn, 145
Rigidity, 32
Road Rage, 102-103

S

SAD, 39
Salt, 54
Saturated fats, foods high in, 52
Seasonal Affective Disorder, 39
Selective serotonin reuptake
  inhibitors, 110
Self-defeating blunders, 98
Self-hypnosis, 201
  effects of, 202
Self-righteousness, 97-98
Self-statements, coping, 32-33
Senate Select Committee, 53
Serenity prayer, 172
Serotonin, 38, 62
Shift work, problems correlated
  with, 183
Shock absorbers, 142
  social, 79

Shoulder shrug, 119
Shoulds and should nots, 40, 97
Sigh of relief, 204
Sleep regimen, 186
Sleep, 177
  better, techniques leading to,
    194-195
  doctor recommendations, 188
Social experiment, 33
Social phobia, 28
SSRIs, 110, 111, 114
St. John's Wort, 116
Stages of sleep, 179
Stay healthy, three factors, 173
Stress,
  adapting to, three stages, 21
  chain of events, 14, 23
  chronic, resulting problems
    of, 19
  conditions and characteristics,
    13
  controlled, 21
  prolonged, symptoms, 18
  reducing diet, guidelines, 53
  short term, two ways of
    dealing with, 21
  super, 141
  symptoms, 9-10, 16
  tolerance, 172
  uncontrolled, 21
  what is, 17
Stretching, 117-118
Super stress, 141
Supervision,
  balancing the stress of, 146
Supervisor, personality, 143

Surveillance,
  surviving high-tech, 133

SWAT, 99

T

TCAs, 110, 111

Teasing, 98

Tech Stress, 123-126
  surviving, 123

Tech work, humanizing, 129

Technology, getting involved, 35

Telecommuting, 136-137
  ways to limit, 137

Television, 149-153

THC, 68, 69

The Ed Sullivan Show, 106

The Stress of Life, 21

Thermal biofeedback, 205

Time management,
  what it requires, 172

Time off, should you take, 149
  manage your, 171

Title VII, 71

Toke, just a little, 67

Transcendental meditation, 207

Tricyclic antidepressants, 110

12-step programs, 42

Type-A, 22

Type-B, 22

Tyrant, 76

U

Ultimatums, 98

V

Valium, 109, 110

VDT, 124, 125, 126, 130
  declines, 124, 127,128
  ways to maximize skills,
    126-127

Violent characteristics, 93

Visual Display Terminal, 124

Vitamin B, 53, 55
  deficiencies, 51
  sources of, 51

W

Ways to combat depression, 45

When Anger Hurts, 93

Whining, 98

WMSD, 128

Work, types of, 12

Workers' Compensation
  Appeals Board, 155

Workers' compensation, 153
  what to expect, 156

Workplace,
  human conflict in the, 79
  the changing, 14

X

Xanax, 109

Y

Yankee Group Survey, 123

You message, 101

Your perspective, questions to ask, 86

Z

Zen, 107

ABOUT THE AUTHOR

DR. JOHN ARDEN IS THE Director of Training for Psychology and Social Work for the Kaiser Permanente Medical Centers in Northern California. In this capacity he oversees 20 different training programs in as many medical centers. He is also the Director of Training at Kaiser Permanente Vallejo, where he previously served for many years as the Chief Psychologist and currently leads the job stress treatment program. He has taught in colleges, professional schools, and universities and is the author of four other books.